NO WAY TO TREAT A LADY

Lady Alicia shivered in delicious anticipation of Lord Ian Cairnyllan's joyful reaction when she told him, "We are suited to each other . . . Ian."

Lord Cairnyllan merely shook his head, as if his worst fears had been confirmed.

Alicia frowned at him, waiting. Didn't the man understand that the most eligible woman in London had practically proposed to him? Finally, unable to keep silent, she said, "Don't you see that I'm suggesting we marry."

"Marry?" he exclaimed. "Are you daft? I shall find a virtuous girl from my own country."

And Lady Alicia Alston, known as "the Ice Queen" to the legion of men who had fruitlessly courted her, felt herself for the first time melt—not with passion but with rage . . . a rage for revenge. . . .

The Impetuous Heiress

SIGNET Regency Romances You'll Want to Read

THE IMPETUOUS HEIRESS

by
Jane Ashford

A SIGNET BOOK
NEW AMERICAN LIBRARY

SIGNET TRADEMARK REG. U.S. PAT. OFF. AND FOREIGN COUNTRIES
REGISTERED TRADEMARK—MARCA REGISTRADA
HECHO EN CHICAGO, U.S.A.

SIGNET, SIGNET CLASSIC, MENTOR, PLUME,
MERIDIAN and NAL BOOKS
are published by New American Library,
1633 Broadway, New York, New York 10019

First Printing, June, 1984

1 2 3 4 5 6 7 8 9

PRINTED IN THE UNITED STATES OF AMERICA

One

"Oh, Roddy, don't *you* begin to be a dead bore," drawled Lady Alicia Alston, gazing out over the great hall of Perdon Abbey with a distinctly jaundiced eye.

The Honorable Roderick Massingham, second son of the Earl of Murne, sighed and leaned an elbow on the carved oak bannister of the ancient minstrel's gallery. The one trouble with Alicia, he thought, was that she was so deuced easily bored. It took all a fellow's time just to keep her mildly amused, and he couldn't remember when he had last seen her really laugh. Often, struggling to hold his own against her lightning wit, he wondered if the thing was worth the effort.

Watching Alicia's discontented profile, Roddy decided yet again that it was. Though he had known her for most of his twenty-six years, he had never become accustomed to her beauty. It struck him every time he looked at her. It was because of her mother, of course. The Duke of Morland, Alicia's father, had startled London society by bringing home the dazzling daughter of a Swedish count as his bride, and Alicia had inherited her silver blond hair, ice blue eyes, and slender willowy body that was entrancing despite her height. It would help if she weren't so tall, though, Roddy thought. It was difficult to impress a woman who stared one straight in the eye. And Alicia was far too accustomed to giving orders and being obeyed. That was her father in her. Roddy nodded wisely to himself. Old Morland was known for his high-nosed ways. It was all very well in him, but he should have kept a tighter rein on his daughter. When she used that certain tone of voice, Roddy often caught himself doing what she commanded before he thought, and only afterward wishing that he had protested first.

But they were all that way, the group of young fashionables who surrounded the *ton's* most spectacular deb. Or hardly that now, Roddy corrected himself. Alicia had been out for, what, six years. She had refused several very eligible offers. Ned Trehune was making a cake of himself, calling her "the Ice Queen" since she turned him down. And if she wouldn't have a belted earl . . . Roddy sighed again. One of the throng of suitors who hung about Alicia had to win her. Was it so ridiculous to believe that it might be he? With a sinking suspicion that it was, he looked up, to find Alicia watching him.

"You look just like a stuffed frog, Roddy. What *is* the matter?"

When she cocked her head at that angle, and lowered her eyelids just that way, Roddy thought, he always felt an inutterable fool. "Nothing's the matter. Thinking."

Alicia's beautifully molded lips curved upward. "You, Roddy?"

"What are we doing this afternoon?" he answered hurriedly. "Didn't old Perdy say something about a riding party?"

"Perdy! *Why* did I let him cajole me into coming here? I might have gone to Vienna to visit Papa at the

Congress. But no, I listened to Perdy, who promised all sorts of new amusements. I should have known better."

"Well, you should," agreed Roddy. "After all, Perdy."

They contemplated their host, Viscount Perdon, in disgusted silence for a moment.

"How is the duke?" inquired Roddy then, recalling his manners.

"Oh, you know Papa, always terribly busy." Alicia's tone was airy. She didn't want Roddy inquiring too closely into her imagined trip to Vienna, for Papa would probably not have been pleased to see her there. On his increasingly rare stops in England, between diplomatic chores, he welcomed her company for as much as three days together, but at the end of that period they invariably began to irritate one another. Each was too accustomed to his own way, and entirely *unaccustomed* to opposition. "Did you see that chaise arrive a little while ago?" she added to change the subject.

"The fusty one with the old-fashioned boot? Yes. Prime cattle, though."

"Who was it? Some fresh guests, I hope. I am so tired of the same faces—here, in London, in Leicestershire hunting."

Roddy professed ignorance. "With that outmoded carriage, can't be anyone from town."

"Provincials? That would be unlike Perdy. But they might amuse us."

He shrugged. "Could find Perdy and ask him."

"Oh, I don't know." Alicia stared into the great hall again, frowning. She was horridly bored. Her friends bored her, Perdon Abbey bored her, and the thought of another Season in London, soon to begin, bored her most of all. She had seen everything the *haut ton* had to offer. She had received its adulation as her due and become the undisputed leader of the younger smart set. But she was weary of that as well. From the moment of her birth, Alicia had gotten whatever she wanted, with only her mother's premature death to mar her happiness. Now, at twenty-five, she had run out of requests. "I suppose we may as well."

"What?" Roddy had been racking his brain for amusing ideas, and he had been just about to suggest they search out some of the others and organize a game of croquet. He felt the plan was weak, and when Alicia spoke just as she might have if he had mentioned it, he was almost afraid she had been reading his mind.

"Look for Perdy," she replied impatiently, starting toward the stairs.

"Oh . . . oh, right. He's probably in his study."

Alicia made a derisive noise.

"Well, he can sit there, can't he?"

"He can *sit* wherever he likes. But to call it a 'study' when Perdy hasn't the brains of a lap dog . . ." She shook her head, lifting the flounced skirt of her blue morning gown to walk downstairs.

They found Viscount Perdon asleep in a red leather armchair. Its back had been turned toward the door in a pathetic attempt at concealment.

"Perdy," said Alicia, shaking his shoulder sharply. "Wake up. It is eleven o'clock in the morning!"

With a snort, as if surfacing from the ocean depths, their host jerked upright. "Wha . . . oh, Alicia. Must you do that? You frightened me nearly out of my wits. It's very bad for one's health to wake suddenly, you know. Causes——"

"It's even worse to sleep at midmorning." She eyed Perdy's plump, sandy-haired form and unbuttoned waistcoat. "After an *immense* breakfast."

"Now, Alicia." The viscount looked apprehensive.

"Perdy, *why* did you ask me here? To drive me mad with boredom?"

"Now, I say. Lots of people to amuse you. Roddy." He indicated him. "Jane Sheridan. You like her. Jack Danforth. Emmy Gates."

"I know who is staying, Perdy." Alicia's light blue eyes narrowed as she surveyed him. There was something odd here that she hadn't realized before. Perdy was notoriously lazy; he rarely invited guests, and when he did, they were a selected few of his male cronies, who could be relied upon to look after themselves and not to expect prodigies of entertainment.

The current house party was unprecedented. She should have seen it as soon as he began pressing her to visit. It was quite out of character. "What are you up to, Perdy?"

"M—me?" But he quailed under her gaze like a rabbit before a fox.

Intuition led her to add, "Does it have anything to do with those people who arrived today?"

Perdy went pale, gaping at her. "People?" he echoed in a strangled voice.

"Who is it, Perdy? What have you done?"

Their host swallowed, groped for his handkerchief, and passed it over his face. "Not my fault," he muttered.

"What isn't?" Abruptly, Alicia sat on the arm of his chair. Her voice became cajoling. "Now, Perdy. Tell us."

Roddy stifled a laugh as the viscount raised his head hopefully. "It was my Aunt Sophia."

"Yes?" Alicia was the picture of sympathy now. "What did Lady Corwin do?"

"Said I must invite my cousins, second or third cousins really, and see that they met some people. Give them a push, you know."

"So it is your cousins who have arrived?"

Perdy nodded, looking dejected. "It's what put me out, so I thought a bit of a nap . . . *he's* bad enough. I've met him before. But *she* . . ." He mopped his brow again. "It ain't my fault, Alicia. I couldn't help it. You know Aunt Sophia."

"Umm." Alicia seemed lost in thought.

"You will stay out the week, won't you?" added Perdy anxiously. "It's only two more days."

When Alicia said nothing, Roddy replied, "Of course we will. All of us."

"So there is a he and a she," mused Alicia. "Who are they, Perdy?"

"The Earl of Cairnyllan and his sister Lady Marianne MacClain. And their mother, of course."

"Cairnyllan? I don't think . . ."

"Scotland," muttered Perdy unhappily.

Alicia eyed him. "And what is so bad about them?"

"Him, I said. I've never met Marianne. Though from what Mama tells me . . . but she can't be worse than Cairnyllan. *He* makes my blood run cold."

"Good heavens, is he a hunchback?"

Perdy stared. "Of course not. Nothing like that in our family. Who told you so?"

Alicia's blue eyes twinkled. "No one. But if he makes your blood run cold . . ."

"Well, he does. But it's his eyes, not his back. He

looks at me as if I were a dead cat—several days dead."

This raised his hearers' eyebrows. None of Perdy's friends thought him keen-witted, but he was well-liked.

"He don't care for the *ton*, you see," added Perdy in explanation. "Disapproves of fashionable fribbles." He nodded as if remembering some incident. "Very cutting, his tongue."

"Indeed?"

Both men, instantly wary at this familiar exclamation, turned to gaze at Alicia. She was smiling slightly.

"What are you planning?" asked Roddy.

"Planning?"

"Don't play the innocent with me. I know that look."

"Roddy! I was simply thinking that we may find this visit quite amusing after all. You must tell me *all* about your cousins, Perdy." She smiled down at him, and Perdy met her eyes with worried fascination.

"Well," he began, "Marianne is to come out this Season, you see."

When the Perdon Abbey house party gathered for a light luncheon at one, there was a distinct feeling of excitement in the air. Roddy and Alicia had alerted their friends to the new arrivals, and everyone was curious to see them. But even more, they could all see that Alicia was plotting something. From long experience, they knew that this meant, at the least, interesting developments ahead.

The newcomers were the last to appear. The others had already gone in to the cold buffet in the dining room, and thus had a good view of the three when they entered a few moments later. Many would have been daunted by the battery of appraising glances thrown their way, and indeed, the small older woman shrank back slightly. But no one was looking at her. The man and girl framed in the double doorway claimed everyone's attention.

Both had stunning red hair, and both were dressed in passable style, though by no means in the height of fashion. But there the resemblance ended. Ian MacClain, Earl of Cairnyllan, was a large man—tall, with great shoulders and arms and well-formed, muscular legs. His face was reddened by the sun, and his blue eyes were startling against his skin. They, like everything about him, seemed to crackle with vitality. He looked as if he would like to tear off his neckcloth and stride outdoors, where he would clearly be more at home. He gazed back at the group around the table with contempt, and none of them imagined he was pleased to be at Perdon Abbey.

His sister, on the other hand, looked overjoyed. She too was built along generous lines, but her deep bosom and curve of hip appeared slight beside the earl's bulk, and one chiefly noticed large, dark blue eyes in a pale oval face, a pert nose, and invitingly sensuous lips. She came forward first, holding out both hands to Perdy.

"Hello, cousin. My room is splendid." She gazed about, smiling as she spoke, with no trace of a Scottish accent, and it was obvious she was gauging her effect on all of them.

Perdy shuffled uncomfortably and freed his hands. "Ur, hullo, Marianne." He paused, as if uneasy about this form of address, then plunged ahead. "Want you to meet my friends." He muttered names rapidly and inaudibly. "Lady Marianne MacClain," he finished, gesturing vaguely. Then, realizing that he should have presented the girl's mother first, he flushed. "And Lady Cairnyllan," he added in a louder voice, "my, er, aunt?"

"Second cousin once removed," corrected Marianne with no trace of embarrassment. "Ian and I are twice removed."

This was too much for Perdy. "Ian MacClain, Earl, you know, Cairnyllan," he blurted, and then turned determinedly to the buffet.

The earl had moved forward, escorting his mother, and now he nodded to the group without enthusiasm. He looked at them, thought Alicia, as if they were some unusual, and not particularly attractive, breed of livestock. But she noticed that when his eyes passed over her, they showed a momentary flicker. She smiled inwardly. Since the age of fifteen, Alicia had enjoyed men's reactions to her beauty, which she knew was extraordinary. Lord Cairnyllan was unlikely to stammer or gape, but she was sure that in a moment or two he would maneuver his way to her side and try to capture her attention with his best conversational gambit. She felt a familiar quickening at the idea; the game of flirtation was one of the few things that still amused her, though she very seldom encountered a worthy partner.

But the earl did not approach her. He stayed beside his mother, filling a plate for her and then sitting near her at the table. His attention appeared to be divided between Lady Cairnyllan's comfort and Marianne's behavior, which obviously concerned him. Alicia did not even catch him in surreptitious glances.

Puzzlement over his amazing attitude preoccupied

her through the first part of the meal. It was not until Roddy, who'd been casting more than surreptitious glances in Marianne's direction, stopped to peel an apple for her that Alicia cocked her head and lowered her eyelids slightly, saying, "Lord Cairnyllan, you are Scotch?" At her tone, the young people around the table looked up expectantly.

"A Scotsman," replied the earl. "Scotch is whiskey."

Alicia blinked. She wasn't used to being curtly corrected, and the man had not even seemed to notice her mockery. Or, if he had, he obviously did not care a whit, which was astonishing. Then she realized that, living so far from town, he probably had no notion who she was. "What part of Scotland?" she added.

"The highlands. You wouldn't know the place."

The way he said "you" goaded Alicia into an uncharacteristic rejoinder. "Perhaps I would. My father, the Duke of Morland, has an estate in Scotland."

MacClain shrugged. "'Tis on the western coast."

"But what town?"

"Cairnyllan," he answered, as if to an idiot.

Perdy gasped audibly, and the others looked shocked. Alicia was speechless; no one had ever spoken to her so rudely in her life.

"It's a tiny village a million miles from anywhere," put in Marianne quickly. "No one could have heard of it. There are only a few cottages and masses of sheep. And our house, of course. The nearest neighbor is fifteen miles!" She looked around for sympathy, and got it. "You can't imagine how dreary it is in the winter."

"I can," said Roddy, who was enjoying his exposure to Marianne's charms.

Lord Cairnyllan scowled, and his mother looked uneasy.

"You don't agree with your sister?" said Alicia.

"I do not."

Unlike Marianne, he had a very slight Scottish lilt to his voice, Alicia realized.

"Oh, Ian likes nothing better than to live at the end of the earth. He hates London," said Marianne.

"And if I do," responded her brother, "perhaps I have reason." His vivid blue eyes fixed Marianne for a long moment.

To everyone's surprise, the girl flushed deeply and looked down. There was a brief uneasy silence, then she raised her head again and tossed back her lovely hair. "*I* can't wait to see it," she said defiantly, and smiled at Roddy.

He took her lead. "This is to be your first visit?"

"Oh yes. I am to come out, you know. I'm half sick with nerves."

Though this was patently untrue, it was the sort of remark the group was accustomed to, and the conversation became general as they discussed the approaching Season. Neither of the older MacClains joined in, and Alicia was unusually silent, her attention repeatedly drawn to Ian MacClain. She couldn't quite make him out. She had met people before who professed contempt for the *haut ton* and its activities, but they were most often those who had been excluded from its ranks. Lord Cairnyllan's birth and breeding did not put him in that category; he might lack polish, but he was far from the gawky provincial she had expected. And Perdy had told her he had a good deal of money. She could see no reason for his attitude, or for his treatment of her. Perhaps she had been a trifle patronizing, but she hadn't spoken more than two sentences. And most men turned her teasing aside with a smile, vastly pleased with the attention. His rudeness piqued and angered her.

Watching him talk with his mother, she scanned his face. His russet eyebrows jutted out to shadow his eyes; his cheekbones were high beneath them, and his nose slightly arched. One didn't realize at first how attractive he was; the impression of controlled power was too strong. But she saw now that it was accompanied by an indefinable grace, a quality unlike her own, or Roddy's sophisticated ease. It was the grace of strength and unconcern for others' opinions. Alicia found it intriguing.

At that moment, Lord Cairnyllan looked up and encountered her gaze. She didn't look away; she was no blushing schoolgirl, and she was curious about his reaction. Their eyes, she saw, were nearly the same color. But that did not make them at all alike. She knew from her mirror that hers were a cool, speculative blue, while those she gazed into were bright with energy and impatience.

She held them. Cairnyllan, who had at first seemed surprised, raised one red eyebrow. His mouth curved slightly upward, though not in a smile, and he slowly surveyed her from her silver blond curls to her slender arms lying along the table. His expression was appreciative, but it held none of the deference to which Alicia was accustomed.

He looked at her as one might a beautiful, but flawed, work of art. She was all very well, his gaze seemed to say, but of no real significance. Alicia was astonished and annoyed: by what right did he assume such superiority? When their eyes met again, both pairs held an unmistakable challenge, and Alicia felt a thrill run through her at the thought of showing Lord Cairnyllan precisely how wrong he was.

Luncheon finished, Roddy suggested croquet, and the young people moved toward the French doors to the lawn. Lady Cairnyllan declared her intention of lying down for an hour and then visiting Perdy's mother, their titular chaperone, who joined them only for dinner. Lady Cairnyllan had been obviously scandalized by this information, which annoyed Alicia. When they had all known one another since nursery days, what could it matter? Then, glancing at Marianne MacClain, she wondered. Marianne had taken possession of Roddy's arm, and was leaning against him and gazing up into his face in a very marked manner.

Lord Cairnyllan saw it too. He opened the dining room door for his mother and bowed her out, but he turned to join the croquet party himself.

Alicia followed him onto the lawn and watched with him while the others chose mallets and balls from among those a footman had brought out. Even Perdy was persuaded to play, rather than escaping to his armchair and a nap, as was his custom after all meals. Marianne MacClain was plainly delighted by the activity, and her enthusiasm was contagious.

"Your sister is a very lively girl," said Alicia when the game had started and only she and Cairnyllan remained on the sidelines.

He started, as if he had forgotten she was there, then frowned. "Yes."

"And lovely. She will make a great hit in London."

"No doubt." His tone conveyed his low opinion of that accomplishment, and the idea also seemed to increase his concern about Marianne, for he kept his attention on the croquet ground where Marianne sent Roddy's ball flying into the yew hedge and crowed with laughter.

Alicia, piqued, searched her mind for some subject that would gain his attention. She had never encountered this problem before, and it took her a moment. Cairnyllan still did not look at her. "It's a pity you had to leave Scotland at this time of year, when it is beginning to be so beautiful."

He turned, and seemed to really see her for the first time. "I find it beautiful at all seasons," he answered, but his voice held speculative interest as well as contradiction.

"We all love our home country best, I suppose. Whenever I go back to Somerset, I feel that." Amazingly, Alicia saw that she was losing his attention again. She had never had to make an effort to interest a man before. "Why did you come?" she asked bluntly, her famed address thrown to the winds.

He turned back, startled. "What?"

"If you love Scotland so, and hate London, why come? I suppose your mother could have managed your sister's comeout."

He shook his head. "Hardly."

Alicia, who was not particularly interested in Marianne MacClain, again sought a subject. She remembered something Roddy had said. "You breed horses, I suppose."

This time, she caught his interest. "How do you know that?"

Alicia followed up her advantage. "It's obvious."

"Is it?" His blue eyes narrowed a little. "You saw my team, did you?"

Disconcerted by his quick understanding, Alicia merely nodded.

"Ah. You won't find another such matched set."

She smiled a little. "I shall tell Lord Peterborough so, and Ottley. They may dispute it."

Cairnyllan shrugged, dismissing two of the leading lights of the Jockey Club without a qualm.

"Perdy has organized a riding party for tomorrow morning," added Alicia, ruthlessly sacrificing her host, who, she knew, never rode unless he had to. "The country is not so exciting as Scotland, perhaps, but it allows a good gallop."

"Unfortunately, my horses are being brought down by slow stages."

"Oh, Perdy will lend you a mount." Seeing his contemptuous glance at Lord Perdon, she added, "Or I will."

He raised his eyebrows. "You?"

Alicia, who had received her first pony at three and was renowned for one of the finest seats in England, met his skeptical gaze. "I. Indeed, I have a young horse I should like to see you try. I am only worried that he is not up to your weight, but perhaps he may be, after all." She eyed him measuringly.

Cairnyllan looked startled, and amused. "You fancy yourself a judge of horseflesh?"

This was the opening Alicia had been aiming for. "A rank novice. I leave the running of Morlinden almost entirely to Jenkins. He is a genius at it."

"Morlinden? You have some connection with . . ."

"It is our racing stable," she interrupted with careful innocence. "And since Father is so often abroad, I help Jenkins to run it."

For the first time, the earl looked at her with genuine interest, and Alicia felt a thrill of triumph at having broken his arrogant reserve. As over the luncheon table, their eyes met, and the tension between them rekindled at a heightened level. "Might I see this promising animal?" asked the earl.

"Of course." And, taking the arm he proffered, Alicia led him through the gate in the hedge and along the gravel drive toward Perdy's stables.

As she dressed for dinner some hours later, Alicia's thoughts lingered on the afternoon just past. She had much to think about. She could not remember when she had enjoyed herself more, and she could not understand exactly why this should be. She and Cairnyllan had duly examined Whitefoot, and he had admitted her good judgment. Then they had walked on the lawns, and their conversation had drifted to other matters. But whatever they talked of, Ian MacClain maintained his superior attitude. He appeared to believe that he was the sole authority on every question. And his low opinion of town dwellers was unshakable.

Alicia did not spend a great deal of her time or brain power thinking about men. They were a necessary part of the human race, she would have freely admitted, but until today, she had viewed the sex with a measure of contempt. Since her teens, they had been making fools of themselves over her, apparently believing that absurd compliments, reckless antics, and brooding glances would inevitably win her heart and hand. Several of the more courageous, who had actually tried their luck, had discovered the falseness of this premise. She had unhesitatingly refused every offer. Indeed, she could not imagine herself married to any of the men she knew. If they weren't young and idiotic, they were dull, or unattractive, or unbearably self-satisfied. A few, like Roddy, were simply childhood friends who were too much like brothers to think of as husbands.

And yet, she expected to marry. Until today, she had somehow taken it for granted that she would, despite the fact that she had as yet discovered no suitable partner. But the Earl of Cairnyllan had shaken her complacent avoidance of this problem, even while he infuriated her.

He was by no means foolish. He offered no compliments and certainly showed no signs of trying to impress her. He simply conversed with her with considerable intelligence, making it clear that he was more interested in her responses than her beauty or consequence.

Not, Alicia thought, that he was unaware of her beauty. She struggled to explain him to herself. He responded to it, as she did to his attractiveness, on some silent level. It was as if the fact were obvious, and there was no need to mention it.

At this point, Alicia sighed in exasperation at her inability to analyze her feelings, and noticed her maid's set expression. "I'm sorry, Rose. What did you say?"

"I said, if you don't stand still so I can button your gown, you will be late for dinner, Lady Alicia."

Alicia grinned at her, and did so. A moment later, Rose draped a cashmere shawl over her elbows and stood back while Alicia surveyed herself critically in the long mirror. It seemed very important that she look well tonight, and the glass told her that she did. She had chosen an evening dress of midnight blue satin trimmed with silver piping at the neck and short sleeves, and Rose had dressed her pale hair *à la* Diane, threaded with dark blue ribbon. A diamond pendant of her mother's completed the toilette to Alicia's satisfaction. She smiled a little, watching her full lips curve in the mirror, then laughed. "I'll do."

"You look fine as a fivepence, Lady Alicia," replied Rose.

Alicia laughed again and went downstairs, coming into the drawing room last and greeting the group with such a dazzling smile that Roddy Massingham nearly dropped his quizzing glass into Lady Perdon's low-cut bodice.

They went in to dinner soon after, Lady Perdon presiding with her usual sleepy imperturbability. Glancing from Perdy to his mother, Alicia was again amused by their similarity. It was clear where their host got his plump, sandy-haired physique, his pleasant disposition, and his incurable laziness. Lady Perdon's gown was all the crack, but her expression suggested that she would rather be curled up with the latest novel and a box of chocolates than presiding over a fashionable dinner.

Looking down the table, Alicia intercepted a severe glance passing between Lord Cairnyllan and his mother. At first, she wondered if they had quarreled, then she realized that both were expressing disapproval of their hostess. She turned to Lady Perdon again, trying to see her with the eyes of an outsider rather than those of a girl who had grown up treating her as a delightfully unrestrictive aunt. Her gown *was* rather low considering her ample bosom, she supposed. When she bent forward to flirt with Jack Danforth . . . but anyone could see it was no more than a game. She felt annoyed with the MacClains again, particularly Ian. How dare he judge in that odious way?

Alicia spent a great part of her meal frowning into

her plate, utterly intimidating the young men on either side of her, and it was not until the ladies rose to leave the table that she recovered her animation. Had any of her friends met her eyes just then, they would have been certain that mischief was afoot. For Alicia had decided that Ian MacClain must be taught a lesson. He was an extraordinary man, but his smugness was insupportable. She would shatter that, and then . . . a smile curved her lips as she entered the drawing room.

The younger girls gathered about the pianoforte, and Lady Perdon went off to fetch a shawl, refusing all offers of assistance. Alicia suspected she meant to nap. However, as this left Lady Cairnyllan alone by the fire, it served her purpose very well. Alicia joined her on the sofa.

"I hope you have recovered from the fatigue of your long journey," she said.

"Oh, yes. So kind," murmured her companion in a soft, fluttering voice.

"Have you been to London before?"

"Not since my own comeout, more than thirty years ago." Lady Cairnyllan sighed.

Alicia thought how little her children resembled her. Their father must have been a large ruddy man, she concluded, for Mary MacClain was tiny, with dark brown hair and gray eyes which were still very lovely. She did not look at all like Ian's mother.

"A long time," Alicia said, suddenly sympathetic.

"Oh, don't misunderstand," protested Lady Cairnyllan hurriedly. "I never wished to come. I am very happy in Scotland. Now that Alex is gone . . . I mean . . ."

She trailed off, and Alicia wondered again at the contrast between mother and children. She could not imagine the younger MacClains talking in such uncertain tones. If her husband was anything like her children, Lady Cairnyllan's life must have been tumultuous indeed, Alicia thought.

"I was hoping to organize a table for whist," said Alicia then. "Will you join us?"

"Oh, I . . . no, I don't play."

She seemed so distressed by the idea that Alicia frowned. "Some other game, perhaps?"

"No, no."

Before Alicia could pursue the subject, as her curiosity urged, the door opened, and the gentlemen joined them.

Ian MacClain came directly to the sofa, and when Lady Perdon rejoined them a bit later, he skillfully separated Alicia from the two older women and led her to a pair of armchairs further down the room, somewhat apart from the others. Alicia smiled slightly at his directness, almost ready to abandon her scheme.

"Your sister has a lovely voice," she said when they were seated. Emmy Gates was playing a ballad on the pianoforte, and Marianne was singing.

"She does that," he agreed, watching Marianne briefly before turning his full attention on Alicia.

They looked at one another. Once again, Alicia had the sense of unspoken things passing between them. Under certain circumstances, she realized, one need not put a feeling into words.

"You are here alone?" asked Cairnyllan rather abruptly.

"Alone?" She gazed at him, puzzled.

"You have no older relative or . . ."

"Oh, you mean a chaperone." Alicia cocked her head and smiled. "Cousin Lavinia stayed at home with her dogs, as she knew Lady Perdon would be here."

"Ah." He gazed disapprovingly at their hostess, who was showing Jack and Roddy the steps of some complicated figure for the quadrille.

"She is a thoroughly nice woman. And I have known her all my life." Alicia's voice had sharpened.

"She may be. But as a chaperone, she is somewhat lax, is she not?" He inclined his head in the direction of Jane Sheridan and Willie Morgan, who had retreated to a window embrasure and were deep in conversation, their heads very close together.

Alicia started to inform him that Jane and Willie were engaged, and were undoubtedly discussing their wedding, which was set for the following month. But she pressed her lips together again, eyes sparkling with annoyance. Lord Cairnyllan was uncommonly arrogant, to make assumptions about people he had met only this afternoon. Let him think what he liked, and find out later what a prating fool he had been!

He noticed her expression. "We are rather old-fashioned in the highlands, I fear," he said coldly.

"One might almost say gothic," she retorted.

"Alicia," called Roddy from across the room. "Come, let us try that duet again. Mari—Lady Marianne has never heard it."

Alicia rose and went to the pianoforte, her resolve renewed. Lord Cairnyllan watched her walk away with relief. He had almost been tempted to change his opinion of London misses this afternoon, but Lady Alicia had reminded him in time of their standards of behavior. He too rose, and went to give his arm to his mother, who was on the point of retiring.

For some reason, Alicia felt relieved when he was gone. This was nonsensical, she told herself, when she was planning to give him a sharp lesson. If he chose to talk so disparagingly of the *haut ton,* it would treat him accordingly.

She immediately proposed cards again, singling out Marianne MacClain. Though the girl seemed reluctant at first, she was convinced when the other young people followed Alicia's signal, and in a few moments a number of them were sitting down to a game of piquet.

When Alicia proposed stakes, Roddy raised his eyebrows. She almost never gambled—insisted it was a dead bore—and if she did, it was for small sums. Tonight, however, she appeared to have altered her habit. Meeting her eyes, Roddy abruptly saw what others had noticed some time before; Alicia was in the midst of one of her pranks. There was nothing for it but to go along.

Marianne was a poor cardplayer. Very soon she had lost the small amount of money in her reticule and was scrawling notes of hand in a round childish script. Roddy nearly objected when Alicia explained this process to her, but Alicia quelled him with a sharp glance.

Marianne lost yet again. Jane Sheridan left the table, frowning at Alicia, and the latter shifted a bit uncomfortably under her gaze. Alicia's anger at Cairnyllan was dissipating, and she was wishing she knew how to manage the cards so that Marianne might make up her losses and end the play. The girl was looking very uneasy. Alicia was about to declare the game over in any case when Ian MacClain returned to the drawing room.

Lady Perdon had retired, leaving the cardplayers alone. Cairnyllan started to nod a greeting, then saw what they were doing. One glance at the scattered bits of paper and Marianne's worried face told him all, and Alicia, watching him, was so shaken that she drew in her breath. Lord Cairnyllan was furious; there could be no doubt of that. His great hands clenched and unclenched, and his vivid blue eyes blazed with anger. Alicia waited for the inevitable explosion, ready, if not eager, to defend herself.

It did not come.

Astonished, Alicia watched the man subdue his obviously formidable temper. She saw him take several deep breaths and slowly relax his hands. His face fell back into impassive lines, and only the spark in his eyes gave any clue to his feelings. Strolling forward with a bland negligence fully worthy of White's, he paused behind Marianne's chair. "Taking a flier?" he asked.

His sister started violently, dropping her cards face up on the tabletop, and twisted to gaze at him, frightened and pleading.

"I beg your pardon," was his only response. "I have spoiled your game. Let me make amends by taking Marianne's place." With subtle strength, he practically lifted Marianne from her chair and set her gently aside. Seated, he looked slowly from one to another of the players. "I apologize; you must deal again."

An almost visible tremor went around the table. Alicia felt a thrill of excitement that overbore her contrition. What a powerful personality he was. She had never met anyone like him.

The new hand was dealt, and the play began. It was immediately evident that Cairnyllan was a far finer player than his sister. Indeed, his skill outstripped any at the table. In less than an hour he had recouped Marianne's losses and begun to increase her little store. He played one more hand, betting heavily and accepting notes from each of the others, and when he had won it, stood abruptly. "I believe that is enough," he said, his voice hard.

"You are a splendid player, sir," ventured Alicia, greatly impressed.

"I learned at Cambridge, for just such occasions as this," he replied harshly. "I was determined never to endure them again."

"Again?" Alicia was very curious.

"It's late. Are you ready to go up, Marianne?"

His sister merely nodded, seeming close to tears, and he offered his arm. They started out, then Cairnyllan paused. Turning, he took their notes from his waistcoat pocket, tore them across, and flung the fragments on the table. In the next moment, the MacClains were gone.

"Phew!" exclaimed Roddy when the door shut behind them. "I feel as if I hadn't breathed for an hour."

The others nodded.

"I say, Alicia . . ."

"I know, I know. I went too far. I shall apologize tomorrow." Alicia was lost in admiration.

Roddy gaped. He hadn't expected any such admission. Indeed, he had never before heard Alicia admit she was wrong.

"Wasn't he wonderful?" she added, and rose to stride out of the room, leaving her friends speechless with amazement.

Two

The riding party gathered on the front lawn after breakfast, Perdy looking as if he wished he could disappear. Alicia had put on her dark blue riding habit, which she knew became her admirably, its tight bodice molding to her slender frame. Marianne was resplendent, though a bit subdued, in crimson.

Alicia went to the groom, who was holding both her favorite mare and the young horse, Whitefoot, she had promised Cairnyllan. "Are you ready to try him?" she called.

"I am that." The earl took the horse's bridle and ran a hand along his nose. "I'll be a bit heavy for you, lad, but I shan't push you hard."

Alicia admired the man's russet hair against the sky. "I want to apologize to you for last night," she said.

He shrugged as if to dismiss the subject. "I never supposed *you* had induced Marianne to gamble. It is, I believe, chiefly a male vice." He eyed the men in the group with disdain.

Alicia hesitated, tempted to escape blame by confirming his theory with her silence. His tone had been so contemptuous, and she found she valued his opinion, after last night. But she couldn't. Her friends did not deserve such treatment. "Actually," she said, trying to keep her voice light, "I suggested the game. But it got a bit out of hand."

Cairnyllan looked at her, his amiable expression fading, then turned away to mount without a word. Alicia felt very low as her groom helped her into the saddle.

The sky was partly overcast, with gray clouds streaming in close order across it and a brisk wind, as they all mounted up and turned toward the long avenue and the front gates. Alicia and Cairnyllan, the best riders, took the lead, reining in their fresh horses, then letting them dance a little down the graveled drive.

Alicia drew in a deep breath and threw back her head. This was better. She had been feeling pent-up in the house, she realized. She was used to a great deal more exercise than Perdy planned for his guests. At home, she rode every day, and often walked in the afternoon. Passing the wrought iron gates, she turned her horse's head left and let her out into a trot. There was a splendid ride in this direction, she knew, providing plenty of opportunities for a gallop. Surely Lord Cairnyllan would forget his anger in the joy of it.

They rode along a narrow lane between high hedges and through the tiny village of Perdon, with its scattering of thatched cottages and stone bridge over the stream. From the blacksmith's came the rhythmic clanging of hammer on metal. Beyond stretched fields and a ridge of low hills crowned with trees. The path Alicia had chosen led up and along this for some miles before curving back toward the back of Perdon Abbey park. She urged her mare forward and reached the summit first, pulling up to wait for the others. The view was pleasant rather than dramatic. More fields spread out below, and they could see several other villages to the east. But the path was good, and the small height gave the illusion of distance and intimacy.

Cairnyllan stopped beside her and leaned over to pat Whitefoot's neck. "How do you like him?" asked Alicia, determined to converse.

"He is becoming used to me. I think we shall get on well enough."

"Care to try his paces?" Alicia indicated the path before them.

"Is this a good place?" The earl eyed the terrain doubtfully. The way appeared smooth and easy, but he could not tell when it might plunge down the hill or cross one of the narrow ravines he had noticed further along the ridge.

"Afraid I'll outpace you?" Alicia's mare curvetted, and with a sudden laugh, she gave her her head, thundering off in a full gallop.

Cairnyllan hesitated only a moment before using his heels on Whitefoot and following. The rest of the group watched them pound up a slight incline and then disappear over its rim. "Neck or nothing," murmured Roddy. "That's Alicia."

"Are we going to just *sit* here?" exclaimed Marianne MacClain, who had recovered her spirits in the open air. Then she too spurred her mount to a gallop.

Perdy groaned audibly, but the others were already after her, and he was forced to kick his large, sleepy-looking roan to a surprised trot.

A good way ahead, Alicia was still laughing. The air streaming past her face and the feel of the mare racing under her were wildly exhilarating. She had left everyone behind and was flying along the top of the ridge. Twice, they had leaped narrow defiles, little more than cracks in the hillside but deep and over-grown with thorned blackberry. She felt as if she could go on riding this way forever, away from the world and completely free.

The sound of hooves made her glance back. Cairnyllan was catching up. Alicia's pale blue eyes lit, and her smile became mischievous. She bent a little more in the saddle and kicked the mare to yet greater speed. Happily, the horse extended her neck and ran.

Together, the two riders thundered along the path. Trees and undergrowth flashed by. They leapt anoth-er tiny ravine—first Alicia, then Cairnyllan arching up and over and landing at full gallop. Alicia's laughter floated back as she held her lead, and the sound brought a grim smile to the earl's ruddy face. He bent lower, but he did not close the short distance between them.

Finally, Alicia pulled up beside a massive oak, and he swung in beside her. They were both breathing quickly, and when their eyes met, both smiled. "How dare you ride that way sidesaddle?" wondered Cairnyllan. "I certainly wouldn't want to try it."

She laughed. "I have ridden so all my life." Her smile turned reminiscent. "Though I used to go astride as well, when I was younger."

He raised one eyebrow, but replied merely, "You have the finest seat I have ever seen in a woman."

"Or a man?" she retorted. "I managed to beat you."

"I didn't want to founder your horse." He sounded amused. "If I had one of my own . . ."

"Oh, of course." She taunted him a little.

"And you had a good ten yards start," he added, beginning to be nettled.

"Shall we try it again from here?" Alicia gazed into

his eyes challengingly. She still felt immensely excited, and she realized now that this was not entirely due to the gallop. She had enjoyed winning the race, as she always did, but the presence of Ian MacClain had somehow intensified the sensation. Looking at him now, his ruddy hair brilliant in a shaft of sun and his blue eyes glinting, Alicia was abruptly flooded with a surge of desire. She thought of kissing him, and a thrill shivered through her.

Alicia had been kissed before, twice, in fits of great daring that she had later brushed aside, along with the gentlemen so favored. It had been an interesting experience, one that she was glad to have had but was disinclined to repeat. But watching Cairnyllan's face, she was suddenly certain that with him it would not be the same at all.

The earl seemed to sense the change in her thoughts. He looked slightly startled at the heat in her eyes, then his own flickered and, at the same time, hardened a bit, conveying an equally intense response. They remained very still for a long moment, eyes locked, then Alicia took a shaky breath and wheeled her mare into a gallop again.

This time, Cairnyllan was right behind her. Alicia could see Whitefoot's head in the corner of her eye, and her heart began to pound in rhythm with the hoofbeats. She found it difficult to breathe, and her mare, feeling the uncertainty in her hands, stumbled a little over a rock in the path. Alicia pulled her head up, and they recovered, but the hesitation had allowed the earl to come abreast.

Side by side, they raced, throwing brief glances at one another. Both bent low and urged their horses forward with knees and thoughts, intent on the contest between them.

Alicia was certain she was pulling ahead again when the widest ravine they had yet encountered loomed before them. It was at least six feet to the other side, she estimated, perhaps more. She could take it, of course, but . . . reluctantly, she started to ease the mare back from her headlong gallop, to prepare for the jump. Then she saw that Cairnyllan was making no such prudent move. He was going to attempt it flat out. She let her hand drop again, then quickly changed her mind. She couldn't be sure of making the jump unless she slowed. And neither could he, she thought irritably. He seemed to have forgotten his worries over her horse.

Cairnyllan pulled ahead, and Whitefoot launched out over the ravine. Alicia caught one glimpse as he seemed to falter, then she herself was flying up and landing on the opposite side. Her mare stumbled slightly, then they were galloping along the path again.

After a moment, when the earl did not come up with her, Alicia turned. She saw Whitefoot some yards behind, his bridle dragging, slightly favoring his left forefoot. At once, she wheeled and raced back to the ravine.

Cairnyllan was in it. He had just picked himself up, in fact, and was brushing at the sleeve of his riding coat. Luckily, he had landed in a spot free of thorns, but he would have to push through a great clump of blackberry to get out.

"Are you all right?" called Alicia.

"Yes." His tone was curt, and he sounded angry.

"Good," Alicia snapped, and turned back to reassure the shaken animal. After a few moments an angry exclamation came from the ravine, and Alicia looked again at the earl.

Despite stern self-admonition, she began to laugh. He looked so funny standing there scowling, his head not even reaching the level of the path.

"Very amusing, I've no doubt," said MacClain, the Scottish burr of his R's intensified. "Suppose you give me a hand up."

Alicia stifled her laughter and surveyed the situation. It would not be easy getting him out. The ravine was small but very steep. She would have to dismount. Sliding to the ground, she searched for a branch but found nothing. There were no large trees nearby. Finally, she crouched above him and extended her riding crop for him to grasp. It was not the most stable position, but the earl seemed likely to explode if she did not do something quickly, and she felt sympathy as well as amusement at his plight. How she would hate to be in it!

Cairnyllan grabbed the end of the riding crop and started to climb, but, in his impatience he pulled far too hard, and in the next instant, Alicia had tumbled forward into his arms and both of them were on the floor of the ravine in a heap.

"You blundering idiot," he roared, trying to untangle himself from her mass of skirts and sit up. "Why didn't you hold on?"

"Because you didn't allow me to," blazed Alicia, jerking her head and leaving several strands of silver blond hair in a thorn bush. The pain made her even angrier. "I should have known that a man who couldn't make an easy jump would botch his own rescue."

"Rescue, is it? If your damned horse . . ." He paused, too honest to blame Whitefoot for his mistake. Indeed, Cairnyllan might have admitted that the whole thing was his fault for pushing his mount, and that his anger was chiefly at himself, if Alicia had not chosen that moment to say, "Take your hands off me."

Cairnyllan glared at her, their eyes only inches apart, and Alicia responded in kind. Abruptly, they became intensely aware of one another, and their rage dissolved in something as hot, but of a far different character. Alicia remembered her earlier thoughts, and her eyes shifted to the earl's lips. She could feel his arms supporting her. Seeing the change in her face, his blue eyes flamed. He bent his head and kissed her passionately.

Alicia was stunned. The innocent kisses she had exchanged with men she had known from childhood had been nothing like this. Her whole body seemed to turn to jelly, and a physical thrill sparked from her throat to her knees. She brought her arms up and around his neck, giving herself totally to the embrace. Cairnyllan responded by pushing her back until they were lying side by side on the rough grass, his hands roaming over her back and around to cup her breasts. She relaxed beneath him, knowing suddenly that this was what her life had been lacking until now. She had had everything she could desire, except an equal to fire her passions and share them, as Ian was unquestionably doing. He drew back a little, and she murmured his name, fastening her lips on his again.

At this, he threw off all pretense of reluctance. He had had a moment of doubt, wondering if he were taking advantage of an inexperienced girl, but it was clear that Lady Alicia Alston knew what she wanted. He caressed her breast again, and she sighed with pleasure. With eager fingers, he reached for the fastenings of her habit.

At that moment, they both heard the sound of hooves. Then Marianne MacClain's voice called, "Come on! We are poking along so slowly we will never catch them."

Cairnyllan straightened as if stung and pulled away, struggling to his feet and beginning to brush the dust and leaves from his coat. Alicia followed more slowly, regretful, but realizing that they must preserve the proprieties until they could formalize their relationship. She rose and shook out her skirts, retrieving her hat from the bush where it had fallen.

"Hallo," shouted Cairnyllan, ignoring her. "Marianne, here."

There was a pause, then his sister appeared, gazing down into the ravine with astonishment. "Ian! And Lady Alicia! What happened?"

"We took the jump too fast and were thrown," he replied. Alicia eyed him with indignant amusement. *She* hadn't, she wanted to say, but it was probably best not to go into details. "Get the others to help us up," Cairnyllan was adding, and Marianne nodded, eyes large, before turning away.

There was no time for talk; the whole group arrived in a moment, and they were immediately involved in the rescue. By the time Alicia had struggled out of the defile and remounted, she was hot and scratched and very annoyed, and wanted only to get home and have a bath. There would be plenty of time to talk to Ian, she thought, and the idea was so attractive that she smiled despite herself.

But there was, she found, no opportunity at all. She went immediately to her room on their return and rang for her maid. Though the mishap had kept them much later than they meant, and it was just past time for luncheon, Alicia refused to hurry. She ordered a bath and a tray and spent a leisurely two hours setting herself to rights, frequently falling into fits of smiling abstraction that quite puzzled her maid, who had known her nearly all her life.

When she went downstairs again at midafternoon, no one was about. Ian had probably looked for her, she thought, and given up when she did not come for such a time. She walked through the lower rooms, hoping to encounter him, but she found only Roddy, taking desultory shots at the billiard table and looking bored. He welcomed her eagerly and suggested a game.

"Not just now. Where is everyone?"

"The girls are still in their rooms. I think Perdy is too, actually." He grinned. "Hiding from you and the chance of more exertion."

"And our Scotsman?" Alicia tried to sound casual, but she wasn't certain she succeeded.

"With his mother. Said he was going to sit with her till dinner."

For a moment, Alicia was annoyed. Then she realized that Ian probably wished to talk with Lady Cairnyllan about his plans for marriage. She smiled to herself. "Perhaps I will beat you at billiards then, Roddy."

He snorted. "I should like to see that."

"Very well." She held out her hand for a cue.

The whole party gathered in the drawing room before dinner. Alicia had put on a gown of clinging sea green muslin and was conscious that she looked very well. She expected Ian to approach her at once, but he did not, staying beside his mother and watching the others with a curious hostility. She was puzzled, and had started to walk toward them when dinner was announced and Perdy offered his arm.

Throughout the meal, which Alicia found very long, she continued to observe Ian MacClain. He didn't look at her, and for a while she could not imagine why. Then, she suddenly realized that he was probably embarrassed. He had behaved in a most unconventional way this morning—some would say scandalous. Perhaps he was afraid she was offended. Alicia's lips curved; she would have to enlighten him at once.

But MacClain was feeling disgust—with himself for having been lured into responding to Alicia today and, more particularly, with this group of Londoners surrounding him. He had been perfectly right about them; they were libertines and wantons. He was very worried about Marianne, who did not seem to have the strength of character he would have expected in his own sister. What would she do in such society? He shuddered to think, and he had spent most of the afternoon convincing his mother that they should return home at once. But just as he had succeeded, Marianne had come in and nearly had a fit of the vapors when she discovered it. Characteristically, Lady Cairnyllan had swung around to her point of view. How was he to control Marianne without her help?

He felt somewhat better when the ladies left them, though he was still concerned about the others' influence over Marianne. He decided to risk leaving her alone for one evening in order to make a last effort at swaying his mother.

Alicia was astonished when Cairnyllan did not appear with the other gentlemen. And when informed that he had gone up to his mother, who had retired early, she almost gave public vent to her annoyance. Though she stopped herself in time, she was by no means a pleasant companion during the rest of the evening. After a while, even Roddy avoided her, unwilling to endure another sharp set-down or curt rejoinder. And Alicia went to bed in a foul mood, feeling thwarted as she never had in her life. Only her determination to rise early and catch Ian at breakfast prevented her from breaking in on his *tête à tête* with Lady Cairnyllan.

She was washed, dressed, and downstairs by eight, an hour when she knew she should meet Ian and no one else. There had been some remarks about his early rising. But when she asked one of the servants whether he had yet come down, she received the astonishing news that the entire MacClain party had departed for London at first light. "Did he leave a note for me?" she was surprised into asking.

"No, Lady Alicia. They all bade us say their farewells." Seeing her thunderous expression, the butler added, "They apologized for going so early. I understood it was some sort of family business."

"Indeed?" Alicia's voice was icy. She turned away and strode out of the house, automatically taking the path that led to the stables. What was the man doing, she wondered? Why had he gone without a word? Mere embarrassment would hardly urge flight. Or would it? She shook her head. There was something inexplicable here, and she meant to find out what. She would stay until tomorrow, as she had promised Perdy, but then she would see Ian MacClain if she had to go to his hotel. Whatever ridiculous scruples were keeping him from declaring himself would soon dissolve when she told him her own feelings. And then they could startle society with the announcement of their engagement. *How* the *ton* would stare! The thought improved her temper, and she smiled as she told the groom to have her mare ready for a ride after breakfast.

Three

Alicia arrived at her father's London townhouse five days later, having been delayed by a broken axle. As always, when first entering it, she was reminded of her mother, who had died when Alicia was only nine. No other place evoked those flashes of a figure very like the one she saw in the mirror and a voice with an enchanting, exotic lilt. The country place was wholly Alston, but in town, her mother had refurbished and added some objects from her own native land. It was an interesting house, both unconventional and charming.

But Alicia had little time to spare for memories just now. Hardly a moment had passed on her journey when she was not thinking of Ian MacClain. Since she could not conceive of rejection, she remained sorely puzzled about his actions, and more and more eager to meet him and discover his motives. Thus, her first act after changing out of her traveling clothes was to riffle through the stack of invitations that had arrived in her absence. Though she had returned to London two weeks earlier than usual and the Season was not yet in full swing, it had begun, and there were a number of entertainments planned. Alicia scanned the gilt cards with an expert eye, then, after a moment's frowning consideration, chose one and strode to her escritoire. As she dashed off a note of acceptance to a musical evening, her mind was already busy with the question of dress. If the MacClains attended any party tonight, and Lady Corwin had no doubt seen to their entrée, this was the most likely, and Alicia intended to be in her best looks when she faced them.

Her judgment turned out to be accurate. The first person she saw after she had greeted her deferential hostess was Ian. He was difficult to miss. He towered over most of the crowd by half a head, and the stiff, disapproving expression on his face was in marked contrast to the smiles and simpers of the others.

Alicia paid no attention to it. Using all her social skills, she made her way directly to him while seeming to chat without any particular aim. In five minutes, she was there. And since Ian's dour looks and curt replies had driven off the few people who had tried to strike up a conversation with him, she did not have to separate him from a group. "I wish to talk to you," she said. "Shall we step into that alcove?" There was a curtained recess close by, the draperies partially drawn.

Cairnyllan looked as if he might object, then bowed his head and followed her.

When they were alone, Alicia eyed him. He didn't look embarrassed to see her. What was the matter with the man? "You left Perdon Abbey very abruptly," she began.

"It was time to go."

His ruddy brows shadowed his eyes, but she could see that he wasn't looking at her. She frowned. "I expected you to speak to me before you went."

Now, he surveyed her, examining her rose pink silk gown trimmed with silver ribbons, her silver gilt hair piled on top of her head, her rubies. The gown was cut too low for any respectable girl, he thought, and the challenging stare of those pale blue eyes was far too confident. The corners of his mouth turned down, and he started to make a contemptuous rejoinder, but a sudden idea stopped him. There might be one valid reason for her manner. "You thought I should apologize?" he ventured.

Alicia cocked her head. Was this then the problem? That was easy enough to remedy. "You needn't apologize to me for what happened between us. Surely you could see that I enjoyed it as much as you. We are suited to each other . . . Ian." She waited for him to take up this thought and ask for her hand.

Lord Cairnyllan merely shook his head, as if his worst fears had been confirmed.

The silence lengthened. Alicia frowned at him, waiting. Didn't the man understand that the most eligible woman in London had practically proposed to him? He had not been so tongue-tied when they were in one another's arms. Why didn't he speak? Finally, unable to keep silent, she said, "Don't you see that I am suggesting we marry?" Her tone implied he was an idiot not to; she waited for his amazement and gratification.

But Cairnyllan's face did not shift; if anything, his expression became even more forbidding. "Marry?" he exclaimed. "Are you daft? I shan't marry a shameless London wanton who lies down in the bushes with any stranger she meets. I shall find a virtuous girl from my own country, who would die sooner than behave so."

For a moment, Alicia did not even comprehend his words. Her smile remained, gradually becoming fixed and strained. Then, the full enormity of it burst upon her, and she began trembling with shock and rage. Did this . . . provincial numbskull actually believe that she had ever behaved in that way with any other man? Could he be so stupid and insensitive as not to recognize the very special feeling she had for him? *Had*, she emphasized to herself, for now she hated him with all her heart and soul.

"How dare you say such things to me?" she cried.

"Why not speak the truth? Because you are at the very peak of London society? Oh yes, we have heard a great deal about your consequence since we arrived in town. But I care nothing for the *ton*. In fact, I despise it. And now, if you will excuse me." He inclined his head, turned, and left her standing there.

Alicia was so angry that she saw and heard nothing of the party surrounding her. A mist of rage seemed to rise before her eyes, and her breast rose and fell rapidly as her hands clenched and unclenched. All her life, she had been given whatever she asked for, and most times she had not even had to ask. Servants, friends, suitors did their utmost to anticipate her desires and be the first to fill them. In the rare cases when she had wanted the impossible, some substitute had always been found, and she had become wholly accustomed to having her own way. Not that she had been tyrannical or capricious; it had never been necessary to abuse her power, for others catered to her out of genuine love or admiration. Thus, Lady Alicia Alston had never before experienced the deep frustration and chagrin she now felt. And this painful experience was compounded by Cairnyllan's misunderstanding of her, and his contempt. The emotions that washed through her in response were almost too strong to bear.

Alicia remained alone in the alcove for some time,

drawing further back so that no one should see her and come in. Gradually, she regained control. Her anger grew colder, though by no means less intense. Any hurt she might be feeling was completely swallowed up in it. She called Ian MacClain every name she knew, and vowed over and over again that she would make him regret what he had said.

When she came to this point, she felt steady enough to emerge from the recess and stand just beyond the draperies scanning the crowd. There he was, talking to Maria Osbourne as if nothing out of the common way had occurred. He was really the most odiously self-satisfied, arrogant man she could imagine. He obviously had no doubt he was right about her, and about everything else in the world as well. Alicia's eyelids dropped slightly. She would show him his mistake, so thoroughly that he would cringe with shame. And then when he tried to apologize, she would simply turn her back and walk away. The picture pleased her so much that she managed a thin smile.

If she could have heard what Ian MacClain was thinking at that very moment, her smile might have widened, for he was by no means content. By right, he knew, he ought to be congratulating himself on administering a much deserved setdown to a woman whose manners and morals were deplorable. But each time he began to do so, the image of Alicia's shocked and incredulous face rose before him and filled him with unease. Moreover, he felt an increasing disappointment at the knowledge that she was unlikely to speak to him ever again. The memory of their encounter in the ravine recurred, accompanied by an overwhelming rush of loss. Though he sternly tried to shake it off, repeating to himself all his objections to her character and style of living, it would not recede. Indeed, with each passing minute it was stronger. And he had to fight the impulse to go back to her and beg her forgiveness. She might have been his wife, a part of his mind would not stop repeating, and that disreputable part could imagine no happier fate.

But Alicia knew nothing of this, and she watched him through narrowed eyes and plotted revenge. At first, she could not think of a suitably terrible retribution. Then a lovely figure in pale green satin caught her eye, and she turned to find Marianne MacClain in animated converse with Teddy Monroe. At once, she saw what to do. And, this time, he would not best her. Turning, she looked about until she found the man she wanted, then walked across to him with head held high.

"Alicia, my dear," said Lord Robert Devere when she greeted him. "I never thought to see *you* tonight."

"Nor I you. This is not your sort of party."

"One does many foolish things out of boredom, alas."

They exchanged a smile, and Alicia looked over her old friend with great satisfaction. Robert was just what she wanted for this scheme. One of the most polished Corinthians of the day, he was tall with an admirable shoulder and leg, extremely handsome, and unfailingly elegant. His black hair was brushed into a fashionable Brutus; his coat was from Weston and fit him flawlessly, and his hazel eyes sparkled with wit and intelligence.

"Why have you come back to town so early?" he inquired.

"For the same reasons as you, I suppose," she lied.

"Do not say you are as weary of society as I, dear Alicia. I can give you ten years, or almost."

Though she knew it was actually twelve, Alicia smiled up at him. Robert was a close friend of one of her older cousins, and had been teasing her since she was able to toddle after them and make a nuisance of herself. But to the rest of the *haut ton*, he was a *nonpareil*. "I want you to do something for me, Robert."

The twinkle in her companion's hazel eyes disappeared, though he continued to smile. "Really? What?"

"Don't be difficult this time. It's important."

He spread his hands. "Have I refused?"

"No, but you usually do. You are the most selfish person, Robert."

"And you, of course, are the soul of generosity."

"I often do things for my friends!"

"For example?"

"Well . . ." Alicia searched her mind and, appallingly, could not think of one instance. She frowned. "You have driven them right out of my head."

"Of course," agreed Devere ironically. But seeing Alicia's eyes, he added, "What is this thing you wish me to do?"

Alicia hesitated, still annoyed, then turned and gazed out over the crowd. "You see that girl in the far corner, the one with the red hair?"

"Yes," he replied warily.

"She is very lovely, is she not?"

"Alicia, if you have some new notion of matchmaking, I warn you that I . . ."

"Not at all. Quite the opposite."

"I beg your pardon?"

"I don't want you to marry her. I just want you to flirt with her shockingly."

Devere looked startled. "To . . ." He glanced at Marianne. "She looks very young. I am hardly welcome among the debs, you know, Alicia. Their mothers warn me off as a hardened rake." He smiled.

"This one will welcome you," she assured him.

"Will she?" Devere met her eyes speculatively. "What precisely are you up to? Who is that girl?"

"Her name is Lady Marianne MacClain. She is from Scotland."

"MacClain," he murmured. "A connection of Cairnyllan's?"

"You know him?" Alicia was surprised, and not entirely pleased.

"I met him this evening. He seemed a very odd sort of man."

"What do you mean?" Robert was looking at her as if he saw far too much, but Alicia could not help asking.

"He appeared quite disgusted with the lot of us, yet here he is."

"His sister is coming out this Season. He brought her to town."

"Ah. The lovely Marianne?"

Alicia nodded, wishing Robert were not quite so acute. He suspected something of the truth, she was sure. She braced herself for further questions.

But they did not come. Instead, Devere paused a moment, as if considering, then said, "All right, my dear. I will attempt to engage the child's interest. It will be a woefully unfair contest, you know. How far am I to go?"

"As far as you are allowed to," answered Alicia bluntly.

Again, Lord Devere looked startled. "You say that as if . . ." He broke off, and turned to look at Marianne again. "I wonder if I shall be sorry for this," he murmured.

"Why should you? You are always flirting with someone."

"*Not* with chits fresh out of the schoolroom, my dear Alicia, and most particularly not those with large and bellicose older brothers."

"Oh! I had not thought . . ."

"I didn't suppose you had. But you needn't worry. I can manage the situation."

Of course he could, Alicia told herself. Robert was up to anything. But she still felt an unexpected uneasiness as she met his sardonic gaze.

"Will you present me?" he added.

"Present . . . ?"

"To Lady Marianne."

"Oh. Oh yes." But she didn't move.

"Come, come, Alicia, don't have second thoughts. They are invariably pedestrian and abominably dull. I'm certain you have a good reason for your request."

Alicia's rage revived, and she nodded. "Come along."

"Bravo," murmured Devere, and he strolled after her across the drawing room floor.

Four

"But really, Alicia, you ought to have summoned me at once," said Lavinia Alston for the fourth time. "If I had known that you were back in town, I would of course have cut my visit to Elizabeth short. I . . ."

"It isn't of the least consequence, Cousin Lavinia," interrupted her charge. "The Season has barely begun, and I have gone out only twice. In any case, I am getting beyond the age for a chaperone."

"Nonsense!"

"Everyone knows me, and . . ." Alicia broke off as she remembered Ian MacClain's conclusions about her. Would he have judged her differently if Lavinia had been there? Could she perhaps be mistaken? With a quick shake of her head, she dismissed the idea.

Her companion watched her face. Lavinia Alston had always considered herself a forceful woman, and her schoolmates and fellow inhabitants of Woosley-on-Marsh, where she had lived most of her adult life, would undoubtedly have agreed. But since coming to live with her remote third cousin Alicia seven years before, her certainty had begun to waver. She did not understand exactly how it came about, but Alicia usually managed to do just as she pleased, even when

Lavinia disapproved. It was not that she was afraid of the girl; indeed, she had a great deal of affection for her. And she was twenty years older and firm in her opinions. But somehow, this never seemed to suffice. They didn't quarrel, but some force in Alicia inevitably overbore all other considerations. Often, Lavinia recalled her life in Woosley with fond regret. It had been very comfortable. She had had enough money, though not the lavish supply she could now command, and she had been quietly content breeding her King Charles spaniels and exchanging gossipy visits with her neighbors. She might have refused when the Duke of Morland had descended upon her in a dazzle of magnificence and requested her services for his daughter. But of course she had not been able to resist. And the seven years had certainly included exciting moments. Whatever else might be said about Alicia, she was never for a moment dull.

Yet today, Lavinia sensed some change. For one thing, it was quite uncharacteristic of her to break off in the middle of a sentence and stare frowning into the distance. Even in the few hours she had been back, Lavinia had found her cousin curiously abstracted. What had happened, she wondered, in the week Alicia had been in London? "Where did you go?" she asked, hoping for some clue.

"Go?" Alicia turned puzzled blue eyes on her.

"You said you went out twice."

"Oh. A musical evening and a rout party."

Lavinia waited for her to add that they had been sadly flat, and when she did not, looked at her even more closely. The look of boredom in Alicia's eyes had indeed disappeared—a startling enough development—but it had been replaced by an expression Lavinia could not identify, and she did not find it particularly reassuring. What could Alicia be up to now, she wondered uneasily?

She did not find out. She ventured a few more questions, receiving monosyllabic replies, and then went upstairs to unpack. If Alicia's strange mood persisted, she would make her own investigations.

A morning caller who arrived a half hour later was more forthright, asking Alicia straight out. "For I know you are up to something," she finished. "You *must* tell me all about it."

Alicia looked at her dearest friend with a half smile. She and Emma Monroe had come out in the same Season and formed a lasting bond the moment they met. This hadn't changed when Emma became Lady Winthrop six months ago. Her marriage hadn't seemed to alter her at all. But when she started to tell Emma the story of the last few weeks, Alicia hesitated. She could be sure of sympathy and outrage to match her own over the way Cairnyllan had treated her, but she was suddenly reluctant to expose her feeling even to a dear friend. She was still very upset, she realized then. She had thought the incident safely buried, but Emma's warm interest brought up such a surge of tangled emotion that she couldn't bring herself to speak of it. "Up to?" she replied.

"Alicia! I have been in London only a day, and already I have heard the oddest stories. They say you have befriended some unknown Scottish deb, and that Robert Devere is paying court to her. Robert! And Roddy claims you have been in a foul temper for days and days. He says you snapped his head off at the Ellingtons' rout party. What is going on?" Emma's brown eyes were lit with curiosity and amusement.

"I really cannot be held responsible for Robert's flirtations."

"Hoity toity. And I suppose you were not seen to introduce the chit to him? Oh no. Nor to leave them alone together as soon as you decently could? And Robert never pays court to unmarried girls. You know that as well as I. You and he are up to something."

Alicia hadn't thought her actions so transparent. Her friend's steady gaze made her a bit uneasy. "Perhaps I have decided to play matchmaker. Robert must marry sometime, I suppose."

Emma shook her head in disbelief. Then her smile faded. "Don't you *wish* to tell me? Of course I would not pry into your affairs. But we have always . . ." She broke off, hurt.

This nearly swept away Alicia's resolve. She and Emma had confided every girlish secret; she had followed the progress of Emma's courtship and marriage in minute detail. But somehow, she could not reciprocate now. It was a wholly different matter to be rejected by the man you wished to marry. *Thought* you wished to marry, she corrected herself quickly. There was no longer any question of that. "Really, it is nothing," she said. "How was your visit to the Winthrops'?"

This succeeded in diverting Emma. "Oh, Alicia, it was dreadful. Jack's mother would talk of nothing but grandchildren. I declare, I did not know where to look. And Jack did nothing but hunt with his father, so I was left with her the whole day. All the neighbors trooped through to stare at me as if I were a freak show. I was never so happy to return to town in my life."

Alicia laughed. "Well, at least you have done your duty and need not go back for a while. The Winthrops do not come up for the Season, do they?"

"No."

"Well, then."

Emma stretched her arms. "You're right, of course. I've hardly realized I *am* back, I suppose. Have you seen Jane or Selina?"

They fell into an exhaustive examination of their mutual friends' plans for the Season and chattered at full bore until Emma rose and declared she must go. "Jack will wonder what has become of me. We are to lunch at my aunt's. Do you go to the Sherburns' ball tonight?"

"Yes."

"Then I shall see you there." And with a wave of her hand, Emma went out.

Left alone for the first time that morning, Alicia did not move. It was unlike her to sit in silent thought, but her mind seemed much fuller than usual, and she was in the unfamiliar position of not knowing precisely what she felt. She was sad about her new reluctance to confide in Emma, and slightly uneasy about the gossip evidently starting about herself and Marianne MacClain. But there was something more wrong, something she could not identify. Alicia felt a discontent far stronger than the boredom and impatience with silliness she had experienced over the last year or so. In fact, she was suddenly overwhelmed by the notion that her life was empty. It seemed there was nothing to look forward to except a repetition of the parties, visits, and outings she had tired of already. She might achieve her revenge on Cairnyllan through Marianne, but that wouldn't change anything.

Alicia had a moment perilously close to despair. Her plans seemed pointless and petty, her actions ridiculous. But she didn't allow herself to sink beneath this onslaught. Straightening in her chair, she flung back her head and gazed haughtily at the striped wallpaper. It was just feeling so distant from Emma, she thought, that had brought on this melancholy. She would be all right as soon as she began doing something. And to hasten the process, Alicia rose and went upstairs to decide what ballgown she would wear tonight.

The Sherburns' ball was not one of the brilliant events of the Season, but Mrs. Sherburn had wisely scheduled it early so that her guests would not be lured away by other, more prestigious entertainments. She was presenting her only daughter to society this year and meant to do her utmost to make her a success. She had begged every cousin, godchild, and connection of her family to urge their own friends and family to attend, and as a result, she was highly gratified by the crowd that filled her reception rooms at nine that evening. "There is Lady Alicia Alston," she told her daughter just before they went to open the dancing. "I feared she wouldn't come. You must be very polite when I introduce you to her. She has immense influence among the young people."

"Who is that man she is talking to?" wondered Miss Sherburn. "He is very handsome."

"That is Lord Robert Devere," answered her mother repressively. "He is not a proper person for you to know."

Miss Sherburn's mouth set in mulish lines, though she said nothing.

"My campaign is going very well," Devere was saying at that moment. "Indeed, better than I could have hoped. Lady Marianne is . . . ah, amazingly receptive."

Alicia felt a pang of uneasiness, but she said, "Didn't I say so?"

"You did." Devere eyed her. Alicia looked ravishing, as usual, in a gown of shimmering silvered blue. But she did not seem in her customary spirits. This was becoming more and more interesting. "I must be off. The lady has promised me the first dance."

Alicia merely nodded, but her eyes followed Robert as he walked across the room to Marianne, bowed over her hand, and led her into the set which Miss Sherburn had opened. Marianne looked radiant. She was obviously vulnerable to Robert's practiced charm. Why did this not give her more satisfaction?

"Alicia," said someone behind her.

She turned to face Roddy. "Oh. Hello."

"I asked if you wanted to dance," he added.

"I don't know."

"You really make a fellow feel welcome, don't you?"

"I'm sorry, Roddy. I was thinking. Let's do dance."

They walked out onto the floor together and joined in.

"What's the matter with you, anyway?" said Roddy after a while. "You've been acting strange since before we left Perdy's."

Alicia started a little and gazed at him. This was the last thing she wanted. "I? Nonsense, Roddy. It is all in your head." And she launched into a determined stream of chatter to divert him from such ideas.

The evening passed in a routine that had become all too familiar to Alicia, but she exerted herself to seem the same to her friends, and by the end of the supper interval, she was satisfied that she was succeeding. Even Roddy no longer looked puzzled. And the rest appeared to have noticed nothing out of the way. She was finding the banter and gossip difficult to sustain, however, and rather than joining the dancing after supper, she slipped through the long red velvet draperies and out onto the terrace that ran along the back of the house. A small garden lay below the broad stone balustrade, and the scents of boxwood and verbena rose to meet her. The sky was clear and moonless, and the stars glittered cooly above. Alicia leaned her elbows on the stone and took several deep breaths. It was lovely to stand here in the fragrant silence and listen to the babble of the crowd inside. The contrast made her solitude the more precious.

But even as she thought this, she heard a step nearby, and a tall figure emerged from one of the other window embrasures and walked to the balustrade a bit further down. An evergreen shrub stood between them, so that the newcomer did not notice Alicia. She had recognized him, however. It was Ian MacClain.

To Alicia's annoyance, her heart began to beat faster. She was displeased at having her idyll interrupted, but at the same time, she felt an involuntary excitement at Cairnyllan's proximity. She tried to suppress it, and could not. Unseen, she watched him. He looked dissatisfied and impatient. The starlight cast deep shadows over his face, but Alicia could see his strong fingers drumming on the stone. Outlined against the lighted window, the lines of his body communicated vast, tightly-controlled energy.

They stood this way for several minutes. Alicia was reluctant to move and be discovered, and Cairnyllan seemed happier outside the ballroom than in it. The country dance that had been playing ended, and the babble of voices rose higher. Then the curtains over the window where Cairnyllan had exited stirred again, there was a low laugh, and a man and woman came out very close together. "You see, it is much cooler," said Robert Devere's voice.

"It's lovely," murmured Marianne MacClain.

Alicia stiffened, but before she could react, Ian MacClain had spoken. "Just exactly what do you think you are doing, Marianne?" he asked.

The girl started visibly, and peered into the darkness. "Ian?"

"Indeed." He strode forward and confronted them.

"I was just . . . getting a breath of air. It is terribly hot inside." Marianne sounded both defiant and a bit frightened.

"And I suppose this . . . gentleman suggested a stroll?" His tone was so contemptuous that Alicia drew in her breath sharply.

"Robert Devere," supplied the other. "I did, actually."

Even from a distance, Alicia could see MacClain stiffen and his fists close. But Robert's tone had been supremely confident and unconcerned.

"Let's go back in," urged Marianne, clearly hoping to escape her brother.

"You will go back in with me," said the latter. "And I shall take you directly to Mother."

"I won't. Come, Lord Devere." Marianne turned on her heel and hurried through the draperies. After a moment, Devere followed her. Alicia could imagine his crooked smile.

Cairnyllan blew out his breath and started forward, then stopped, paused, and returned to the balustrade. He pounded on the stone twice with his fist, the picture of anger and frustration, then turned back to the ballroom. Alicia poised to move as soon as he was gone, but even as she leaned a little forward, the glorious song of a nightingale burst from the garden behind her, stopping Cairnyllan and making him look around. Alicia's skirt had swung out of shadow and now shimmered in the starlight. "Who's there?" asked Cairnyllan sharply.

Caught, she came slowly forward, cursing herself for having moved.

She put up her chin and looked at him from beneath lowered eyelids.

"You? You're alone?"

He sounded surprised, and this turned Alicia's embarrassment to anger. "As are you, Lord Cairnyllan."

"How long have you been there?" He didn't wait for an answer. "Long enough. I didn't see you come out. No doubt you find it very gratifying to see my sister learning your corrupt town ways. You and your friends must be greatly amused."

Alicia said nothing. Apparently, he hadn't heard that she had presented Robert to his sister. She found she was glad of that.

"Well, it shan't go further, so you can stop your laughing," added Cairnyllan. "I couldn't keep Marianne from coming to London, but I shall see that she doesn't become like *you*."

The bitterness in his voice inflamed Alicia's anger so that she didn't hear the disappointment that accompanied it. Various replies occurred to her, but she was trembling and did not trust her voice to be steady. Thus, she said only, "You are a fool," before sweeping back to the long windows and into the ballroom. There, a waltz was just beginning, and Alicia scanned the crowd until her gaze met that of an admirer. At once, he approached and begged her to dance. Still raging inwardly, she nodded and they swung onto the floor.

Cairnyllan stayed on the terrace for a while, trying to regain control of his temper. Marianne's indiscretion seemed somehow ten times worse for having been witnessed by Lady Alicia Alston. He longed to throttle them both, but particularly Alicia. As he forced himself to relax, he wondered at this. Why should he care what the woman did? She was less than nothing to him. He had no respect for her type and no interest in her as an individual. Yet the strength of his emotions contradicted him outright.

Pushing the thought from his mind, he too re-entered the ballroom. The sight of Marianne whirling a second time in Devere's arms made him grimace, but it was another couple that caused him to turn his back and stalk to the sofa where Lady Cairnyllan was chatting with two older women. The waltz, he decided, was indeed an immoral dance, as certain commentators had suggested. And Lady Alicia's pliant grace in it was simply another sign of her flawed character. He would not think of her again. But as he took up a position behind his mother, Cairnyllan's eyes persisted in defying him, following a silver-blue-clad figure around the ballroom.

Five

The following day, Alicia called at Emma's townhouse in Berkeley Square to look over the new furnishings she had been accumulating. Emma was doing a complete renovation of the place, which had not been touched, she insisted, since Jack's grandmother died thirty years before.

"What about his mother?" asked Alicia with a smile as they walked through the newly decorated rooms and she dutifully admired shot-silk hangings, Egyptian-style sofas, and intricately inlaid tables.

"She never comes to London. She was telling me when we visited how glad she was to have no daughters to bring out." Emma grimaced. "She practically ordered me to produce four sons, just as she did."

Alicia burst out laughing.

"It is easy for *you* to laugh. You wouldn't find it so funny if she was your husband's mother."

"I'm sure I shouldn't," replied the other, eyes dancing.

"Oh, I suppose it is funny. Come back to the drawing room, and we'll have some tea."

When they had settled there and rung for refreshment, Emma looked around with great satisfaction. "I had no notion what fun it was buying furniture,

Alicia. You should try it. Your house is full of old things."

Alicia surveyed the blue walls, scarlet draperies tied back with gold tassels, and brilliant Turkey carpet. Emma, she thought, had fallen too far under the influence of the Prince Regent's style of ornament. She murmured something which might be taken for agreement, having learned years ago that Emma's enthusiasms were intense but brief.

"It would give you something to do. You are always complaining about being bored."

"Not always, Emma."

The tea arrived, and she paused to pour, looking pensive. "It's true you haven't mentioned it today," she admitted. "Nor when I saw you last. In fact . . ." She eyed her friend closely. "Have you fallen in love, Alicia?"

Alicia almost choked on her tea. "What?"

"I always used to tell you you should, remember? And it would certainly explain the way you have been acting lately."

"I haven't been——"

"Yes, you have. Everyone's noticed it. Even Roddy, though you seem to have diverted him. We've all talked about it."

This disturbed Alicia. She had always enjoyed being the center of an admiring group, but now she realized that her position might have drawbacks as well as advantages. She was not at all eager for such close scrutiny just now. She tried to think of some light answer that would satisfy Emma and turn her thoughts in a new direction.

"Love is amazing," continued Emma dreamily. "If anyone had told me when I first came to London that

I would moon about like a sick calf over Jack, I would have laughed in her face. Why, Jack isn't even very handsome."

Alicia, who had thought this from the first but never dared say it, raised her pale eyebrows.

"But he's wonderful. So jolly and kind and . . ." Emma's brown eyes misted reminiscently, and her lips curved in a secret smile. Alicia watched her with curiosity, and a little envy. She had never heard her friend talk so before, but they had seen little of one another since her wedding. It was only now, in town again for the Season, that they had the usual opportunities to meet. "I wonder what it is," murmured Emma, half to herself, "that makes one man stand out suddenly. You are going along quite happily, flirting with dozens of them, and then you turn and meet his eyes, and . . ." She shrugged. "That's that. It remains only to inform the gentleman—discreetly, of course." Her dimples showed. "It is enough to make one believe in Cupid, like the Greeks. Or was it the Romans?"

Alicia laughed again, but she was interested in spite of her desire to turn the subject. What Emma described sounded very much like what had happened to her with Cairnyllan. Not that she felt anything of the kind now, of course, but it was interesting that their experiences had been so alike. Alicia felt another twinge of envy watching her friend's happy expression. "It is not always so simple," she replied involuntarily.

"Oh no. How dreadful it must be to fall in love and then find the man isn't. And I know I was annoyed when someone I didn't care for followed me about and vowed undying love. I was very lucky." Her inner

smile reappeared for a moment, then her eyes widened and she turned to stare at Alicia. "Don't tell me
that *you* . . ."

"This has nothing to do with me, Emma. I don't
know what can have put the idea in your head.
Perhaps you think so much of love because of your
own situation."

Emma considered this, frowning. "Do you think so?
But you have been different, Alicia, and——"

"I am growing old and crabbed. But I am *not* in
love." It was perfectly true, she told herself. Whatever
she might have felt once, it had died when Cairnyllan
had insulted her.

"Oh, well." Emma looked regretful. "It is too bad.
It would be good for you."

"I doubt it." Alicia could not keep a certain amount
of scorn from her voice. She had seen how good it
was.

"It would. But never mind. You'll see, someday."

Alicia decided it was safest to leave the subject
there, though she felt like protesting again. "Have
you seen the new play everyone is talking of?" she
asked.

"Oh, yes. Jack and I went three nights ago. You
would love it, Alicia. It is very amusing."

"Really? Perhaps I will go tonight. I think Lavinia
spoke of taking a box."

Emma nodded. "I nearly forgot to tell you. I have
been hearing all sorts of things about your friends the
MacClains."

Alicia frowned. "They are the merest acquaintances. But what can you have heard?" She wondered
uneasily if some echoes of her encounter at Perdy's
had filtered back to London.

"Well, I admit I was curious when I saw Robert Devere flirting so desperately. I have always had a *tendre* for him, you know."

They exchanged a grin. At seventeen, Emma had fancied herself madly in love with Devere, who had barely spoken three words to her.

"Of course you know who his father was?"

"Robert's?"

"No, Lord Cairnyllan's."

Alicia shrugged. "Also the Earl of Cairnyllan, I suppose. And also a Scotsman who cared more for sheep than——"

"No. He was Beau Alexander!"

Alicia's blue eyes widened, and Emma nodded eagerly.

"No one connects them, because Alexander was his first name, but they are the same."

"But wasn't he one of the most notorious gamblers and rakes of——"

"Yes. My mother remembers him. It was she who first told me. And then, of course, I asked everyone. Some of the stories! Do you know that he lost a fortune twice over, and then won one back a few months before he died? And they say he once had three mistresses at once, each in her own *very* expensive house, and they met in the park one day—all three!—and there was such a row!"

"It's impossible." Alicia tried to connect the insufferable Ian MacClain with the infamous figure of Beau Alexander, and failed.

"It is strange, isn't it? Do you think that is why Robert is so interested in Lady Marianne? Perhaps she is like her father and——"

"No!" Alicia set down her cup with a crash that

nearly shattered the fragile china. What had she begun? No wonder he hated gambling!

Emma stared at her. "What's the matter?"

"I . . . don't care to hear such stories."

Her friend's eyes grew wider. "What do you mean? You are usually the one *telling* them."

"Well . . . but . . . Marianne MacClain seemed a sweet girl. I'm sure you are mistaken." Alicia knew this sounded weak, but she could think of no better reply. No wonder Cairnyllan hated London and distrusted the *haut ton*, she thought. Fragments of old gossip came back to her—elders expressing pity for the families of men like Beau Alexander, rumors of a public humiliation of his wife at the King's *levée*.

"She is not behaving like a 'sweet girl' from what I hear. She is said to be ready for any mad romp, and very fast."

Alicia's feelings were too confused to answer this. If she had known the family's history, would she have thrown Marianne and Devere together? Guilt rose within her, to be countered by memories of Cairnyllan's insults. He had it coming! Perhaps he had cause for his prejudices, but he was still mistaken. Yet Marianne hardly deserved to be an object lesson for her stiff-necked brother. Her thoughts going round and round, Alicia yearned for solitude. "I must go," she said, rising.

"Now?" Emma gazed up at her.

"Yes. I . . . I forgot an appointment . . . with my dressmaker."

"But you saw her yesterday morning. You were telling me about the blue pelisse . . ."

"A fitting," blurted Alicia. "I will see you again soon, Emma. Good-bye." She rushed out, leaving

Emma staring after her, her mouth a little open. She remained in that pose for a long moment, then leaned back on the sofa with a speculative frown. Alicia might say what she liked, but *something* was wrong with her. And Emma was beginning to form an idea of what it was. Slowly, she smiled, then began to giggle. Much as she loved her friend, it was refreshing to see the imperturbable Alicia so agitated.

For her part, Alicia rode home in a kind of daze. She was trying to understand what had happened to her since meeting Ian MacClain. She *had* been acting strangely; Emma was right. In fact, she thought now she must have been mad. Why had she urged Robert to lure Marianne MacClain? She knew his reputation, better than most, and how much of it was deserved. In her privileged position, she could be his friend without danger of gossip, but no other unmarried girl dared as much. Marianne knew nothing of London, and what if some similarity to her debauched father waited within her? Even as she rejected this melodramatic idea, Alicia decided she must talk to Robert and make him moderate his flirtation with the girl. She could find other ways of punishing Cairnyllan. Or better yet, she would simply forget him altogether. He was not worth such worry.

With these laudable resolves, Alicia descended from her barouche and swept into her own townhouse through doors held by deferential servants. But by the time she reached her bedchamber, she was wondering why her resolves did not make her feel any better. Nothing seemed right lately, and she almost missed the days when her largest problem was how to conquer her ennui.

Lavinia was determined to see the new play that evening, and Alicia allowed herself to be coaxed into accompanying her. She was heartily tired of her own thoughts, in any case. They had an early dinner and arrived in the box Lavinia had secured a few minutes before the curtain. Lavinia leaned out to survey the crowd and nod to those of her acquaintances she had not yet seen this Season. Alicia fixed a smile on her face and sat still. She was too preoccupied to notice when Ian MacClain entered and took a seat in the pit.

For his part, he kept his head down, his expression stiff. He did not feel entirely comfortable about his decision to come to the play. His mother and sister were spending a rare night at home, so that he was not needed to dance attendance, but he could not rid himself of the notion that he was being self-indulgent. His distrust of town amusements told him that he should have stayed away, yet curiosity and a taste for drama had overcome his better judgment. He had always enjoyed reading plays, but he had never before had an opportunity to see one performed. Despite himself, he felt a thrill of anticipation when the curtain rose and the actors appeared.

The play was definitely above the average. Even Alicia found herself caught up in the action. Lavinia was enthralled, and Cairnyllan scarcely moved in his seat until the interval. When the curtain fell again, he sat back with a deep sigh and admitted to himself that he was glad he had come. Watching a play was utterly different from reading it. Perhaps London had something to offer after all.

Looking around the theater, he saw several people he had met in the past few days, but it did not occur to him to go up to the boxes as he saw many of the other gentlemen in the pit doing. He was content where he was. Then he noticed Alicia in a box almost directly across, and his breath caught. Whenever he came upon her suddenly, he had the same reaction; her beauty seemed almost like a blow. Tonight, in a simple gown of pale peach and a glitter of topaz, she stood out from the others in the audience like a jewel among pebbles. Though he knew he should not, he could not help staring.

"Won't do you a particle of good," declared a lugubrious voice nearby.

Cairnyllan started violently and turned to gaze at the young man on his other side. He had fleetingly noticed him when he sat down, and dismissed him with contempt, for his neighbor clearly aspired to the dandy set, which Cairnyllan detested, and he found his strangling collar, profusion of fobs, and padded coat ludicrous. "Were you speaking to me?" he asked coldly.

"Saw you lookin' at Lady Alicia. Just thought I'd drop a word in your ear. Friendly warning, you know."

"Warning?" Cairnyllan's icy tone would have put a more sensitive man to immediate flight.

"No sense in other fellows suffering as I did—do." The slight young man put a hand over his heart and sighed. His large, rather protruberant brown eyes swiveled to gauge his listener, then back to Alicia. The candlelight gleamed in his pomaded hair.

"I haven't the slightest notion what you are talking about," replied Lord Cairnyllan. "Or for that matter, who you are."

"Good Lord. Beg your pardon. Ned Trehune's the name. I believe my misfortune has affected my manners." He looked rather pleased at this idea. When he saw that Cairnyllan was still mystified, he added, "Lady Alicia, you know. She turned me down."

"Ah?" Cairnyllan was interested in spite of himself.

Trehune nodded, then sighed again. "I call her the Ice Queen. That hair, you know, and her eyes can certainly freeze a fellow quicker than . . ." He paused, at a loss for a neat comparison.

"Indeed?" Still more curious, Cairnyllan surveyed his companion. Though ridiculous in his eyes, he was obviously a member of the *haut ton*. Yet his information was wholly at odds with Cairnyllan's own observations. He sought a way to question without arousing Trehune's curiosity. "I had, er, heard that she was a bit . . . fast."

"Alicia?" He shook his head. "Must have been someone else. Oh, she's up to every rig and row in town and knows all the *on-dits*, but she never so much as gives a fellow an opening. And all sorts of them have tried. I don't think she has a heart." He sighed dramatically again.

Cairnyllan was astonished, and not convinced. "I'm certain a friend told me she had been quite indiscreet in at least one instance."

Trehune turned to focus a suddenly sharper brown eye upon him. His dandiacal pose wavered. "Your friend was mistaken. I've known Alicia for years. Everyone has. And they'd all say the same. She's above reproach. I'd advise you to discourage your friend from that sort of gossip. She's pretty well liked, you know. Could get sticky." And with this, he turned back to gazing soulfully up at her.

Cairnyllan followed his gaze, a frown drawing his ruddy brows together. Trehune was serious, he could see that, and he had also seen the deference paid Alicia since he came to town. He had put it down to the general corruption of London society, to admire such a woman, but now his opinion was shaken. Yet how else could he explain the girl's behavior with him? No sane man would call that "above reproach." For almost the first time in his life, Cairnyllan felt confusion and self-doubt. From an early age, he had been forced to support his mother against an unreasonable and libertine father. The issues had been clear-cut, and he had known with a comforting certainty that he was right. This conviction had helped him through experiences most boys never even imagined. And as he grew older, watching over his permanently subdued mother and rebellious sister, he had had no reason to change his mind. He knew what was right and best for them. He understood the world as they did not.

Now, he was forced to wonder if he indeed understood it. Many things in London had seemed odd to him, but Trehune's calm pronouncement was oddest of all. Could the codes of conduct be so different . . . but he knew they weren't. How, then, to explain Lady Alicia Alston's contradictory nature? To Trehune, she was the Ice Queen; to him she had been . . . He turned from the thought; it was too unsettling.

Looking at her again, transfixed by her beauty, Cairnyllan suddenly remembered the things he had said to her on her arrival in town. If he had made a mistake . . . He clenched a fist. He had not. She had lain in his arms like a common trollop. But Trehune insisted . . . Unable to decide, and extremely uneasy in this unaccustomed position, Cairnyllan turned back toward the stage and tried to put the girl from his mind. Whatever the truth, they were nothing to each other. But even when the curtain rose once more, he could not banish her from his mind. And somewhere in its depths, unknown to him, a tiny flame of hope ignited.

Six

Alicia was able to accomplish at least one goal the very next night. She encountered Lord Robert Devere at an evening party, and at the first opportunity beckoned him to her side, happy to see that the MacClains were not present.

"My dear Alicia," he said, bending over her hand. "Breathtaking, as usual."

She brushed this aside. "I must talk to you about something."

He raised one dark brow and waited.

"It is Marianne MacClain. You must end your flirtation with her."

His eyebrow rose another fraction. "I beg your pardon?"

"You heard me, Robert." Alicia was impatient. "It was a mistake. You must end it."

"You were the one who *began* it, Alicia."

"I know that, but . . ."

"But now you have changed your mind?"

"Yes." She met his hazel eyes squarely.

"Why?"

"That doesn't matter. I just . . ."

"It does. To me." Seeing her look of surprise at his tone, he added, "What do you think I am, Alicia?

Your lapdog? To be ordered one way, then the other, at your whim? I agreed to flirt a bit with the MacClain chit because the idea amused me, and I was curious as to why you requested it. Those things still hold. Moreover, I find Lady Marianne quite charming, not the least like a debutante." He smiled slightly and repeated, "Not the least," in a way that made Alicia very uneasy. "I intend to enjoy the connection as far as I am allowed, as you suggested."

"But Robert . . ."

"You have become quite conceited, you know, my dear. Do you honestly believe that you need but command, and we will all fall in with your wishes? Your position is not so grand as that."

"Robert, I made a mistake. I admit that. I did not know certain things, which have made me think that . . ."

He chuckled. "So you have heard that she is Beau Alexander's daughter? Interesting, is it not? I did not make the connection myself at first, but now that I have, it is plain that Lady Marianne has something of her father in her. What spirit the girl shows!" He smiled reminiscently again.

"What do you plan?" asked Alicia uneasily.

"Plan? You make this sound very sinister. I 'plan' to continue my customary habits—enjoying to the fullest whatever life may cast in my way. I believe Lady Marianne feels the same."

"She is only a child."

His eyebrow rose sardonically again. "Marianne MacClain? On the contrary, my dear Alicia, she is far more mature than you. Do you know why her brother finally consented to bring her to London?"

"So that she might have her comeout," faltered

Alicia, seeing from his expression that there was more.

Devere shook his head. "He refused her that until she was the cause of a duel between two young sprigs in their neighborhood. I believe the fathers requested that she be removed from their vicinity."

Alicia swallowed, a little shocked in spite of herself. "It needn't have been her fault. Young men are often foolish."

He smiled. "You should become better acquainted with Lady Marianne. I wouldn't be surprised if she not only engineered it, but watched from the sidelines, clapping her hands with glee."

"Robert!"

"Oh, take a damper, Alicia. You are becoming a dead bore. What's happened to you lately? I shall do precisely as I please about young Marianne, and that is the end of the matter."

She frowned up at him. She had always thought of Robert as a friend, but she realized now that they had never exchanged more than banter and gossip.

"Come, you are making too much of this. Let us go and speak to our hostess. She will be wondering what I have said to make you look so." He offered his arm, and Alicia hesitated, then took it, trying to summon a smile. It wouldn't do to let everyone see her unhappiness, and add fuel to the speculation already circulating about her. But she felt far from easy, and very sorry indeed that she had been so foolish as to meddle in anyone's life.

The MacClains came in soon after this, and Alicia watched Devere go up to them and separate Marianne from her mother and brother without apparent effort. Lord Cairnyllan did look slightly grim, but he made no move. What must he feel, wondered Alicia, entering the houses, the very rooms, where his father had played out his disastrous career? No wonder he viewed London with hostile eyes, particularly now that the connection was becoming known. Alicia thought of her own background. Everyone knew and respected *her* father, and often spoke kindly of him to her. Her mother too, though less familiar, had been well liked. She had been welcomed into society and made much of from her earliest appearances. How different it would have been had her father been a Beau Alexander.

Alicia had continued to gaze at Cairnyllan as she thought these things, her expression compassionate. Now, he happened to turn and meet her eyes. At first, he seemed surprised. Then, an intent expression crossed his face, and he returned her regard with equal interest. It was as if each were seeing the other for the first time. The look held. Cairnyllan wondered which Alicia Alston he was observing, the reckless girl he thought he had encountered, or the Ice Queen he had heard described.

Then someone walked between them and each realized the obviousness of his pose. Cairnyllan bent to say something to his mother, and Alicia turned to join a group of her friends nearby. They did not think of coming together. What had passed between them made it impossible.

The party took its usual course. Before ten, a group of young people had convinced the hostess to organize dancing. An older woman played for the couples who gathered at one end of the room. Other guests retreated to cards or gossip; some left for other engagements.

Alicia resisted Roddy's attempt to pull her into the third country dance. She was not feeling festive; she considered finding Lavinia and calling for their carriage, but her cousin was chatting very happily with two friends on a sofa. Rather than pull her away, Alicia slipped through the drawing room doorway and walked along the corridor to a window at the end. Here, it was quieter and cooler, and she could rest a moment before returning to the others.

She had been there only a little while when she heard murmuring voices behind her. At first, she ignored them, thinking that some other guests had had the same idea as she, and not really wanting to talk. But then some furtive quality to the sound made her turn and look. She saw Lady Marianne MacClain and Lord Robert Devere, standing very close and whispering together. Marianne had a garment draped over her arm. At that moment, the girl nodded quickly and shook it out. It was a black domino, Alicia saw. Marianne put it on. Robert offered his arm.

Alicia frowned. What were they up to? Surely they were not going to a masquerade so late. No private party would . . . and then she saw. Devere was going to take Marianne to a public masquerade, and without her chaperone; there was no other explanation for their secretive behavior. Probably they meant to go to the Pantheon itself. How could Marianne be so wildly imprudent? And how did she expect to avoid a scandal? Without considering what she meant to do, Alicia stepped forward. "Good evening."

Devere and the girl whirled, Marianne's hand going instinctively to her throat and the clasp of the domino.

"How are you, Lady Marianne?" said Alicia, to show at once that she knew her identity. "I have hardly spoken to you since we came up to town."

Marianne pushed back the hood. "No," she said a bit breathlessly.

Alicia waited, looking curious.

"Lord Devere was just . . . showing me what one wears to the masquerades. I have always wanted to attend one." Marianne sounded both a little nervous and disappointed.

"Indeed? I do not know whether a private masquerade will be held this Season. We had so many last, did we not, Lord Devere?"

"Far too many," he drawled, not the least discomfitted. "And yet even the most familiar event can be amusing when seen with a fresh companion."

Marianne smiled up at him, and Alicia raised her eyebrows. She was about to make some dampening rejoinder when a deep voice from the doorway said, "What is this?" They all turned to face Ian MacClain, Devere grimacing visibly. "Marianne, I have been looking for you."

"Well, I am right here."

Her petulant tone made Alicia smile slightly. She sounded like a child deprived of some treat.

Cairnyllan's stern gaze took in Devere, Alicia, and the domino that still hung from Marianne's shoulders. "Were you going out?" There was steel in his voice.

"Lord Devere was showing me a domino," replied his sister sulkily.

"Was he?" His gaze brushed the other man contemptuously, then went back to Marianne. "Are you certain that is all? You were not thinking of attending a masquerade, after I expressly forbade it?"

"And what if I was?" the girl exploded. "I am sick to death of your rules and commands. You don't want me to enjoy myself at all. It is perfectly all right to slip into the masquerade for a short time, if one keeps one's mask on and stays with one's own party. Everyone says so."

"Everyone?" He looked at Devere, who merely smiled.

"Yes, everyone! Ask Lady Alicia. She knows what is proper."

Cairnyllan gazed challengingly at her. For some reason, Alicia flushed a little. "Sometimes," she admitted, "parties attend the Pantheon masquerades. But it is not considered quite . . ."

"Oh, not you too!" cried Marianne. "Everyone seems determined to prevent me from enjoying my first Season, but I thought you at least were different. *You* do as you please. I daresay you have been to a masquerade." Before Alicia could protest that indeed she had not, the girl added, "I thought when you presented Lord Devere to me that you were on my side." She looked accusingly at Alicia, whose heart sank.

"You introduced them?" said Cairnyllan in an icy tone. In a rush, all his doubts about Alicia came flooding back. He had made inquiries about Devere since Marianne had shown such a marked preference for his company, and the result had made him both angry and uneasy. Devere was not the sort of man any girl should be acquainted with; there could be no two opinions about that. He had been told so even by sophisticated London matrons. And he had been wracking his brain ever since for a way to separate Marianne from the man without making matters worse. He knew if he forbade his sister Devere's

79

company, she would simply see more of him in defiance. He knew her temper too well. So he had been contenting himself with watching her carefully and trying to think of some scheme.

But with the revelation of Alicia's complicity, all his calm resolutions flew away. She was as bad as he had first believed, and the death of the small flame of hope that had started in his breast was bitter. "Marianne, you will take off that domino and come with me," he commanded.

"I shan't! I am not a child any more, Ian. You cannot order me about in that way. I have waited all my life to come to London, and now that I am here, I am going to do everything!" She spread her arms, the black domino belling out, her red hair brilliant above it. "I am so tired of being hemmed in and bullied. You have been bullying me since I was three, Ian, but that is over now." She laughed. "I will never leave London again. I am going to live here all my life."

Cairnyllan looked grim. "On the contrary, we will leave for Scotland tomorrow."

Devere grinned, and even Alicia could see that this was an error.

"*You* may leave. I don't care. I have friends here now who will take me in. The Congdons would be happy to have me. Anne and I are best friends. Or perhaps I shall find a husband who lives always in town, and then I shall never set foot in Scotland again, Ian."

Seeing that he had goaded her into a flaming temper, Ian tried to fall back. "You are overwrought. Come to Mama now, and—"

"No!" Marianne tossed back her head and turned to Devere. "I think I should like to dance." She held out her hand imperiously.

He bowed. "Delighted. Will you, er, wear the domino?"

Marianne held it out as if she had forgotten it, pulled it impatiently from her shoulders, and threw it on the parquet floor. Devere smiled and offered his arm. As she took it, Marianne added, "It will do you no good to run to Mama, Ian. I shall speak to her tonight in her bedchamber, and she will do as I ask."

They swept through the doorway and into the drawing room, leaving MacClain and Alicia gazing after them. "And she will, too," muttered Ian bitterly.

Alicia said nothing. She had noted the flash of fear that had accompanied the anger in Cairnyllan's eyes, and known that his treatment of Marianne sprang from concern rather than fusty morality. And in this case, he had been quite right. It would have been disastrous for her to attend a masquerade escorted only by Devere. What had been his plans for afterward? Once again, Alicia fervently wished she had never introduced them.

And even more, she wished that Cairnyllan had not found out. His low opinion of her must seem confirmed by this fact, and just when she had been trying to atone for her misjudgment.

Cairnyllan looked up. "Enjoying the spectacle?" he inquired coldly. "Did you hope for such scenes when you presented my sister to your 'friend' Devere? You and he are in this together, I suppose. Does it amuse you to drag innocent girls down to your level? Or are you simply his creature, providing prey for his snares?"

"How dare you?" Alicia gasped. She had been feeling sorry for him and wondering how she could help, but this accusation was so vile that she forgot her sympathy.

"Oh, I dare a great deal, as you will find out soon enough. I will stop at nothing to save my sister from such as you and Devere. Be warned. I am not impressed by your consequence or daunted by his reputation. You have chosen the wrong victim this time!"

"You are mad," she retorted. "I have never heard such an insane rigamarole in my life. Lord Devere is a friend of one of my cousins, and I—"

"If that is the sort of company your family keeps, I don't wonder you behave as you do."

"If we are to talk of *families*, Lord Cairnyllan . . ." But she stopped at the look in his blue eyes.

"So you have heard. I daresay it is one of the *on-dits* by this time. I have noticed that you Londoners are fond of French words. Do you think they hide the real nature of your interests? It is still scandal you talk, whatever you call it. And scandal you live. Stay away from my sister, Lady Alicia." And he turned on his heel and was gone.

Alicia was breathing rapidly, her fists clenched at her sides. But she forced herself to wait and grow calmer before she followed him back into the ballroom. The man was hopeless, she thought. Whatever his father had done, it was no excuse for the kind of insulting stupidity Cairnyllan repeatedly exhibited. She would forget the MacClains, all of them, from this moment forward.

Seven

The following evening, Lavinia and Alicia were promised to Mrs. Julia Beaufort, who had organized a party for Vauxhall. Alicia dressed for it with some care but no great enthusiasm. Mrs. Beaufort was an old friend of her family, and she could not seem to understand that Alicia had long ago left the schoolroom. Alicia did not dislike her—indeed, one could not—but she did object to being treated with amused indulgence at the age of five and twenty. Yet Mrs. Beaufort's invitations and attentions were so well-meant that she rarely refused her.

She did, however, choose one of the most sophisticated of her gowns, a sea-green gauze trimmed with bunches of dark green ribbon. To the matching wrap and slippers, she added a fan her mother had left her. It had come from China and held a delicately painted landscape in various shades of green and gray on its slender wooden panels. Alicia felt it gave her toilette a certain worldly air; surely their hostess must at last notice that she was past fifteen.

They arrived at the Beaufort townhouse at nine, and were greeted in a flurry of lavender silk in the drawing room. Though Julia Beaufort was a large woman, she always moved in sudden rushes, with much expressive gesture. Alicia's father had once attributed her manner to the fact that she had been widowed very young and never chosen to remarry. Certainly if she saw herself as thirty, Alicia had realized, she must see the younger generation as children.

"Alicia, darling!" she cried as she enveloped the girl in a scented embrace. "It's been an age since I've seen you."

"How are you, Aunt Julia?"

"Oh, perfectly well, as ever. But let me look at *you*." She held Alicia away from her ample bosom. "I declare, you are more like your mother each day. And what a sweet gown, dear."

Alicia smiled. She wondered what the extremely fashionable, and expensive, Bond Street modiste who had made the dress would say if she heard it described so. It was, in fact, the antithesis of "sweet," as the two of them had intended. Though not quite unsuitable for an unmarried girl, it was certainly at the limits of what one might wear. Its tiny sleeves and scooped neck showed Alicia's lovely neck and shoulders to their best advantage. But Julia Beaufort saw only what she wished to see. "Thank you, Aunt Julia," replied Alicia, still smiling.

"Come and sit down. The others will be along directly, and we can be on our way. Isn't it exciting? I haven't been to Vauxhall in, oh, two years, I believe. Somehow, I got quite out of the habit."

"Is it to be a large party?" asked Alicia. In her experience, Aunt Julia's guests tended to be ill-assorted.

"No, dear. A dozen or so, I think. I'm sure I asked young Teddy Dent at Almack's last week, and he will make twelve. I thought he would be company for you."

Alicia couldn't restrain a grimace. Teddy Dent was nineteen and just up from Oxford. She had met him once and found him insufferably silly. But before she could find out who else was to join them, the butler announced some new arrivals, and his voice made her go very still.

"Mary!" exclaimed Mrs. Beaufort, rising and surging forward with both hands outstretched. "How divine to see you again." She grasped her guest's hands and held them to her bosom. "When I heard you were in town, I was bowled over. And pleased, of course. I had quite given up ever seeing you here."

Lady Cairnyllan, who was dwarfed by her hostess, seemed to be having trouble formulating a reply. She stammered some acknowledgment of Mrs. Beaufort's kindness.

"And these are your lovely children." She surveyed Ian and Marianne, who stood just behind their mother. "The image of you, Mary dear." She shifted to a penetrating whisper. "Nothing of *him* in them at all."

Lady Cairnyllan, diminutive and dark beside her two tall red-headed offspring, merely looked bewildered. Ian stepped forward and gave his name and his sister's.

When Julia Beaufort had greeted them with equal gusto, she took Lady Cairnyllan's hand again and led her forward. "You must allow me to present an old friend," she told Alicia and Lavinia. "Mary and I came out in the very same Season." She tittered. "Several years ago, now, of course. And then Mary went off to Scotland, and I have not seen her since. But when I heard she was in London, naturally I called at once."

"We have met already," said Alicia, who had found her voice by this time. She smiled at Lady Cairnyllan and nodded, including Marianne but avoiding Cairnyllan's eye.

"Indeed?" Mrs. Beaufort seemed disappointed. "How splendid."

The butler reappeared, ushering in a trio of very young men, and the rest of the guests then appeared in quick succession. Mrs. Beaufort swept her party down to two carriages and, to Alicia's annoyance, seated her between two of these sprigs, who appeared overcome by the honor and hopelessly tongue-tied. Since Marianne MacClain, in the same case opposite her, appeared oblivious to the problem, and chattered happily all the way to Vauxhall, Alicia said nothing. But by the time they arrived, she was ready to talk to even Ian MacClain. He was, at least, intelligent.

Vauxhall was lovely, however, and some of Alicia's impatience dissolved as they approached. They went by boat, her favorite method, and she was as always pleased by the panorama of lantern-hung trees, softly-lighted pathways, and colorful strollers. The lanterns made gilded green haloes among the leaves and here and there lit a bed of red or yellow flowers. Music floated over the water to them, along with a hum of talk from the boxes surrounding the pavillion.

"Oh," gasped Marianne behind her. "Have you ever seen anything so beautiful?"

"Only my present companions," dared one of the young men, whose name Alicia had already forgotten. He bowed to each of them in turn, and blushed. Marianne giggled.

With a sigh, Alicia turned away. They had reached the landing, and two attendants were tying up the boat. Mrs. Beaufort herded them all out and over to one of the best boxes, which she had engaged for the evening.

"Now," she said, settling into a chair after having ordered lavish portions of the wafer-thin sliced ham and other delicacies offered, "the children may dance or stroll about the gardens together, and we can have a good *talk*." Her expression as she looked at Lady Cairnyllan suggested that she meant to discover every detail of the years they had been separated.

Lady Cairnyllan seemed to shrink in her chair. Knowing Julia Beaufort, Alicia sincerely pitied her. Aunt Julia was really kind-hearted, but she did not possess a great store of tact or sensitivity. She often asked questions that made her companions blanch, and pressed for answers when anyone else would have noticed their awkwardness.

"I don't think . . ." began Cairnyllan.

But Alicia was ahead of him. "No, no, Aunt Julia. You can't keep Lady Cairnyllan sitting here all evening. She must have a chance to see Vauxhall, too. If you would care to look around, I would be happy to go with you, Lady Cairnyllan. I think I know the gardens fairly well and can show you the best vistas."

"Oh yes," replied the older woman, looking relieved.

"A splendid idea," agreed Cairnyllan, speaking over Mrs. Beaufort's protest. "I will escort you." He offered his arm, which his mother took, and swept the two of them away before their hostess could object again. As they went, he glanced at Alicia with a grateful expression, though he said nothing.

"Let us start with the Grand Promenade," she added. "It is this way." Leading them away from the boxes, Alicia wished that she had not been so quick to speak. The last thing she wanted was to spend time with Ian MacClain, and from what she had seen of his mother, it seemed unlikely that she would contribute much to the conversation. Why had she put herself in this position? And after her firm resolve of last night? This brought back Cairnyllan's insults, and Alicia's mouth tightened.

"Julia was always so positive," murmured Lady Cairnyllan.

"Was she?" replied Ian, sounding amused. "Did she chivvy her friends about in this way even as a girl?"

"Oh, yes." His mother chuckled softly. "I remember once at a ball. She had no partner—she had been away from the ballroom when the set began—but she simply swept up to Ralph Johnston and *stood* there, looking at him, until he asked her. He said afterward that the look in her eye had made his blood run cold."

Alicia burst out laughing, and Lady Cairnyllan started as if she had forgotten her presence. "Oh! I did not mean . . ."

"I understand perfectly," Alicia assured her. She had heard the genuine liking, along with amusement, in Lady Cairnyllan's tone. "I feel just the same. I love Aunt Julia, but she can be a bit *much.*"

After a moment's hesitation, the older woman returned her smile.

"You know, I always wondered if she insisted that Mr. Beaufort offer for her," Alicia went on. "I remember him as such a quiet, retiring gentleman. Of course, he died when I was very young."

Lady Cairnyllan chuckled again, as if unable to suppress it. "We wondered too. He loved her; that was plain enough. But we could not imagine him getting up the courage to speak. And Julia never waited for anyone. Indeed, it took a good deal of determination to get a word in with her. So . . . But I went off to Scotland before they were engaged." The warmth died out of her voice as she said this, and Alicia saw the light in her face fade, leaving behind lines of sadness. She remembered what she had heard about Lady Cairnyllan's unhappy marriage.

"Did you ever come to Vauxhall in those days, Mother?" asked Cairnyllan, obviously trying to redirect her thoughts.

"Oh yes. It was even more fashionable then. The crowds looked quite different, of course, everyone in wigs and satin coats." Her dark eyes grew dreamy. "What dresses we had then. I confess, today's modes have never seemed truly elegant to me. When I was a girl, my favorite gown was of ivory satin; the skirt was caught up with garlands of roses to show an underdress of cherry stripe. With a hoop. I wore a rose in my hair, too, all in powder, of course. You should have seen us strolling here then, Ian. It was a real spectacle."

"And you were among the loveliest," he agreed with a smile. Meeting Alicia's eyes above his mother's head, he quickly looked down again. She was deeply moved by the pity and love she had glimpsed in his face. In that moment, it was clear to her who had kept the MacClain family serene through its difficult years.

"Oh no," said Lady Cairnyllan. "I was never a reigning toast. But I had a splendid time." She blinked and looked around. "Lady Alicia, I beg your pardon. I am boring you dreadfully."

"Not at all. I am very interested. You are talking of the time when my father and mother first met."

"Yes. I'm sorry I never encountered your mother. I have heard about her beauty and wit. You remember her?"

Alicia nodded, growing thoughtful in her turn. "My strongest memory is of watching her brush her hair in the candlelight. She always insisted upon doing it herself. She had a silver hairbrush, and her hair was nearly silver, too. The light seemed to grow brighter on it, as if it shone of itself." She looked up. "I saw her chiefly when she was getting ready to go out."

"How old were you when she died?" asked the other sympathetically.

"Nine." Alicia felt suddenly bereft, as she had not for years. Seeing Ian and his mother laughing together made her feel the lack of such a relationship in her own life.

Silence fell. Both Alicia and Lady Cairnyllan appeared pensive.

"Did you know Lady Alicia's father?" asked Cairnyllan.

"The duke? Oh, yes." His mother smiled again. "Of course, he wasn't the duke then. He was one of the young bucks. We all thought him very handsome, but my mother warned me to avoid him."

"Did she indeed?" responded Alicia, intrigued. "Why?"

"He was a notorious flirt. And he didn't seem likely to settle down for quite a time. Mama wished me safely married." Her smile wavered again.

Alicia burst out laughing. "Wait until I see him next. Papa, a desperate flirt! How I shall tease him."

"Is he away?" wondered Lady Cairnyllan, smiling.

"He is nearly always traveling on diplomatic business."

"And so it is just you and your cousin? Poor child."

Alicia blinked. No one had ever characterized her

as a "poor child" in her life. Quite the opposite. Cairnyllan too was struck. When he had seen Alicia tonight he had been first dazzled by her beauty, as always, then disapproving of her costume. He had forbidden Marianne just such a dress the day before. Then, with her kindness to his mother, he had begun to doubt again. He could not seem to reconcile her behavior and her appearance.

"Look at that," exclaimed Lady Cairnyllan, and both the young people turned.

"It is one of the Grecian temples," replied Alicia. "There are a number of pavillions and statues scattered through the gardens, arranged in vistas."

"Yes, I know," murmured the other, and Alicia belatedly remembered that Lady Cairnyllan was familiar with Vauxhall. "I was talking of that group ahead of us. The gentleman looks very like . . . but it can't be."

Cairnyllan frowned a little. Alicia gazed at the group. There were several gentlemen among it. "Do you mean Lord Wrenhurst?" When Lady Cairnyllan said nothing, she added, "Or Mr. Browne? Or Sir Thomas Bentham?"

"Is it?" Lady Cairnyllan almost whispered.

Alicia and Ian exchanged a puzzled look. He appeared worried. "Another old friend, Mother?"

"What?" She glanced up almost guiltily. "Oh, it is nothing, Ian. I once . . . that is, we were friends long ago. I daresay he has forgotten all about me after all these years. With his own family and . . . is that lady his wife?" She watched the woman in conversation with Sir Thomas with narrowed eyes.

"No," answered Alicia. "Sir Thomas is not married. There is the usual story of a broken heart in his youth." She started to smile, but frowned instead when she saw Lady Cairnyllan suddenly pale. "What is it? Are you tired?"

"No, no. That is . . . yes, a little. Let us . . . oh! They are turning." Indeed, the group ahead had paused, then begun strolling back toward them.

"Do you wish to go, Mother?" said Cairnyllan, preparing to guide her away.

"Yes . . . no . . . I . . ." They gazed at her in astonishment as she first flushed, then paled again.

"Lady Alicia," said one of the women in the approaching group. "How pleasant to see you."

Alicia acknowledged the greeting, and those of the others. When they waited politely for her to present her friends, she glanced at Lady Cairnyllan, who was staring at the gravel path, then at Cairnyllan, who gave her no help. With a small shrug, she made the introductions.

Sir Thomas's reaction was as marked as Lady Cairnyllan's had been. He started visibly, then stared until recalled by a sense of his rudeness. Fortunately, the chatter of the others covered this contretemps.

The two groups walked together toward the boxes. Alicia, very curious by this time, kept a watch on Lady Cairnyllan. At first, her eyes remained resolutely on the ground. But finally, she glanced up, found Sir Thomas gazing steadfastly at her, ducked her head again, then met his eyes. The look that passed between them then was significant. Alicia became convinced that Lady Cairnyllan was the one who had broken Sir Thomas's heart years ago. Amused, she said as much to Ian, her voice low.

"Nonsense," he replied. "I have never heard anything so ridiculous." But his expression as he watched his mother hesitate, take Sir Thomas's arm, and walk on with him was uneasy.

Alicia did not press him. But she found it difficult not to laugh. The picture of Lord Cairnyllan, flanked on one side by his vivacious sister, who was even now flirting with one of the young men in their party, and on the other by his mother, courted by an older swain, rose irresistibly in her mind.

What would he do if Lady Cairnyllan joined Marianne's camp? The prospect rather delighted Alicia. It would surely drive the overconfident earl to distraction, and perhaps teach him a salutary lesson about his domineering ways. He needed to be shown that his own fiats and opinions were not the last word on everything.

At the same time, however, despite her satisfaction, Alicia found herself feeling a little sorry for him. He seemed so stunned by his mother's defection. Indeed, he looked lost. But a sudden sound and burst of light put his dilemma out of her mind. "Fireworks," she exclaimed. "They are starting the fireworks already. Let us find a place where we can see better." And, without thinking, she took Cairnyllan's arm and practically dragged him to a special vantage point she knew. She didn't even notice the others drop behind.

An explosion of green opened above the trees, followed an instant later by a burst of blue. As they faded slowly, sparks drifting down, a red flowering, then a silver followed. The changing lights illuminated the tops of the trees and the upturned faces around them.

With each new burst, Alicia gave a soft sigh of gratification. She had loved fireworks since she was a tiny child, and she never seemed to get enough of them. They were one of the great attractions of Vauxhall for her.

As yet another multicolored spray of light expanded above, Alicia drew in her breath, and clapped her hands twice. Watching her, Cairnyllan was again mystified. This girl seemed to shift from one moment to the next. Not five minutes ago she had been the worldly London miss, calmly suggesting that his shy withdrawn mother had once broken hearts, and now she was acting like an excited child, absorbed in a show of fireworks and aware of nothing else. Enjoying the play of light along her throat and shoulders, Cairnyllan briefly gave up the attempt to understand anything. She was so beautiful, and tonight, at any rate, she had been so kind. He remembered holding her in his arms, and his jaw tightened. At that moment, he asked nothing more than to do so again.

"Oh, look!" cried Alicia. For the finale, there was a series of bursts, one after another: blue, red, silver, green, red. They spread with soft pops across the night sky, a new color opening before the last had faded. Sounds of appreciation could be heard from all sides.

When the last light had disappeared, Alicia relaxed and wrapped her arms around herself. "Weren't they splendid?"

He nodded. "You're fond of fireworks."

"I adore them. I remember the first time I was taken to see an exhibition. I was two. Papa declares that I cannot possibly recall it, but I do." Her pale blue eyes glowed. "After that, I begged to go at every opportunity. My parents grew quite weary of the subject, I assure you."

He smiled. "I imagine they rather enjoyed your

delight." He pictured the small silver-haired child she must have been.

Startled by the warmth in his voice, she looked up at him. When their eyes met, a current of emotion passed between them. Alicia felt the same instant affinity she had when they met. She longed to step forward into his arms and feel again the excitement she had known there. But she knew what he would think of that. Alicia made herself say, "We seem to have lost the others. Shall we go back?" She kept her voice very cool, despite her feelings, and turned away too soon to see his hand come up and reach toward her. In the next moment, he had stifled this unacceptable impulse, and they walked to Mrs. Beaufort's box without touching.

Yet they remained more in charity with one another than they had been since Cairnyllan arrived in London. Each felt that the new things he was learning about the other made a difference.

The box was empty, but a selection of food and drink had been brought, and Alicia could see Lavinia and Mrs. Beaufort not far off. She sat down.

"Would you care for some of this ham?" asked Cairnyllan very politely.

"Thank you, yes," she replied.

He had started to serve her when they both saw Marianne MacClain. She was out on the dance floor, laughing with her head thrown back and whirling in a waltz with a total stranger.

Cairnyllan's hand froze in midair, and his pleasant expression vanished. "Do you know that man?" he asked Alicia.

She did not pretend to misunderstand him. "No." Reluctantly, she added, "He is not of the *haut ton*."

"I can see that." Throwing down the knife, he moved forward.

"Don't."

"I beg your pardon?"

"Don't draw everyone's attention by dragging her back here. Wait until the set is finished, then speak to her."

"You expect me to leave my sister with that——"

"He can't hurt her. They are in public view. If she should need you, you can easily . . ."

As they watched, Marianne threw back her head again and laughed gaily.

"Need me!" Cairnyllan's tone was bitter. "Not likely."

He sounded so hurt and frustrated that Alicia could not help saying, "I'm sure she looks to you for many things, if not for such close chaperonage as you choose to give."

"If Marianne thinks she can——"

"She only wishes to enjoy herself."

He sneered. "I don't care for the *ton's* idea of enjoyment. And I shan't allow her to be corrupted by it."

Watching Marianne flirt with her partner, who on closer scrutiny appeared to be a perfectly harmless young cit, Alicia almost laughed. "I wonder if it's not the other way about," she replied.

"Do you dare to suggest . . ."

"Oh, take a damper, Lord Cairnyllan."

He gaped at her.

"You are so certain you know everything. You are quite mistaken about the *ton*, you know. Oh, you have reason to be. I don't deny that. And of course there are still a few men, and women, like your father. But they decrease each year. We are not such a despicable set." She smiled up at him.

He gazed at her face, wanting very much to believe her. He longed to forget his responsibilities, take her hand, and tell her he had been a fool to reject her at their first meeting in town. But he could not. "And what of Lord Devere?" he responded. "I suppose he is merely a charming philanthropist?"

Alicia's smile faded. Robert was a problem; she couldn't deny it. Again she felt that unaccustomed twinge of guilt over her part in that affair.

"And you brought them together," he accused, his face gone hard.

"I regret it now," she admitted reluctantly. It was hard to apologize, even this obliquely, to the man who had said so many harsh things to her. But it was only the truth. "I . . . I spoke to him, but . . ."

"About Marianne?" He looked shocked, and when she nodded, his mouth set in a grim line. "I will thank you to . . ."

"I was trying to *help*. And I am quite willing to do more to make amends." She nodded to herself. "That's it. I'll help you separate them."

"No, thank you." He looked away. "I don't require——"

"Don't be stupid."

He gaped at her again. Cairnyllan was by no means accustomed to such constant, and sharp, interruption.

"Are *you* having any success?" She indicated Marianne. "You are handling her all wrong."

"I know my own sister!"

"Perhaps so. But you are not acting as if you did. You put her back up at every turn. You goad her into

97

defiance. If you keep on the way you are going, you will most likely push her into some really imprudent rebellion."

He opened his mouth to reply, then shut it again. He had to admit the fairness of her statement.

"She might be more willing to listen to an outsider, one who has some standing in society. Who better to help you than I?"

He met her eyes. Did she mean that she knew all about such affairs? But again, her argument was valid.

"So?" finished Alicia.

"I should prefer——"

". . . to be in Scotland. We all know that. But you are here and must make the best of it." Alicia was feeling irritated. After all she was offering her help despite all he had done to her. She needn't have. The fault was not all her own; Marianne could have ignored Devere. Alicia rather thought Cairnyllan should jump at her offer rather than complain. Perhaps she would withdraw it.

"Very well," said Cairnyllan grudgingly. "Thank you." He did not look grateful.

Alicia nodded curtly. And they were equally relieved to see Lavinia and Mrs. Beaufort returning to the box, their tongues wagging at a great rate.

Eight

Alicia had decided to make an opportunity to talk with Marianne, but when she thought about it the following morning, she did not see how it could be managed without drawing attention. Alicia had never paid much heed to girls younger than herself; indeed, she had most often sought friends from among the older women. There was already gossip about Marianne, and if she suddenly took her up, it would be remarked. She would have to call at the house the MacClains had hired, she concluded, and if necessary, she would confide in Lady Cairnyllan.

Accordingly, she went there at an hour when most morning callers should be turning homeward again and she was likely to find the family alone. All three were, in fact, in the drawing room when she was ushered in, and Cairnyllan rose at once and made some excuse to take his mother away as soon as they had exchanged greetings. Marianne looked surprised, and Alicia frowned at this too-obvious maneuver, but she was also glad not to have to hint and put off the real purpose of her visit. The truth was, she realized, that she was a little reluctant to face Marianne. Though younger, the girl gave such an impression of maturity and assurance that Alicia doubted her own influence. And when they were seated facing one another, Marianne smiling and curious, Alicia did not know how to begin. "Are you enjoying London as much as you hoped?" she asked to break the silence.

"Oh yes. More. It is just as I pictured it." Marianne's blue eyes sparkled. She was looking very lovely this morning, in a gown of blue kerseymere, the sun slanting through a window to fill her red hair with copper lights. She seemed much older than eighteen.

Alicia felt again that uncharacteristic uncertainty. She didn't know what to do about it, because she had never had to deal with such emotions before. It was unlike her to be uneasy in a social setting, and she could only attribute it to her intention of interfering in another's life. She had never done so before the last few weeks, and she was discovering that her former attitude was a true reflection of her character. But she had promised to try. As she looked up, the resemblance between Cairnyllan and his sister suddenly struck her.

"Did Ian ask you to talk to me?" said Marianne.

"What?" Alicia was so taken aback that she could not even formulate an answer.

"Well, you were talking to him last night, and you have not called on us before, so I thought it likely he asked you to speak to me." Marianne smiled. "Although it does seem a bit indirect for Ian. He usually says what he thinks straight out."

"I, er, I did think perhaps . . ."

"Ian worries too much." Marianne seemed unconcerned by her guest's confusion. "He always has. I suppose that's only natural, but it does put my back up. I mean, why shouldn't I be as sensible as he? We grew up in the same household."

Alicia had recovered from her surprise, and she

found her curiosity about this very self-possessed young lady outweighing her mission. "I suppose he feels responsible for you," she replied, abandoning any pretense of disinterestedness.

"Oh yes. And he is afraid I will turn out like our father, of course." She smiled at Alicia's indrawn breath. "Well, I can't help knowing that, can I? I am not *stupid*. I might feel the same about him if he were not so stuffy." She giggled. "He always has been, since we were children. You should have seen him sitting behind the great desk in the estate office, and listening to the bailiff's report when his feet didn't even reach the floor."

Alicia couldn't help smiling at the vision. But there was something touching about it, too. "He is thinking of your happiness."

Marianne considered. "I'm not sure. Ian would rather I be prudent than happy, I think." She shrugged. "Look at the way he acts."

Meeting her eyes, for one awful moment Alicia thought she knew about the incident at Perdon.

"He is actually enjoying himself quite well in town, but he will not admit it." She grinned. "He has not mentioned going home to Scotland in more than a week, however."

Once again, Alicia could not help but smile back, and she was beginning to wonder what she was doing here. Marianne appeared to understand her brother far better than he understood her. Indeed, she understood almost too much for a girl her age. Then Alicia remembered Devere. "What you say may be true," she admitted. "But if your brother does not know London, others do."

"Yes. *You* do." Marianne looked squarely at her. "Did you wish to say something to me? For I cannot imagine Ian persuading you to come here in this way if you did not."

"You are very perceptive." How, she wondered, had the girl become so? She felt that odd uneasiness again. It was almost as if Marianne were the older, more experienced adviser and she the pupil.

"My childhood required it," responded Marianne. "It was very confusing, never knowing whether there would be piles of money or none at all, or whether one's father would shout obscenities or lavish caresses upon one. The first time I saw my father, I didn't recognize him, you know. I was five years old, but he had not been home since I was two. That time, he shouted." She had been gazing at the floor, but now she looked up quickly. "Why did I say *that*?"

The girls' eyes met, Marianne's anxious and uneasy, Alicia's full of sympathy. "I do not usually volunteer confidences," added the younger girl. "In fact, I never do. But something about you . . . I don't know. It just came out."

"I'm very flattered." And she was, Alicia realized.

Marianne frowned, still concerned, but something she saw in Alicia's eyes seemed to reassure her. "*Did* you wish to speak to me?"

"Yes. I know it seems impertinent, but . . ."

"It doesn't, really." She shrugged. "I don't know why, unless it is because I don't at all mind taking advice from people who know what they are talking about. Ian makes me so furious because he does *not*. He has been in Scotland miles away from everything just as I have. How can he know any more?"

This was so logical that Alicia ignored it. "I wanted to say something about Robert Devere."

"Oh." Marianne cocked her head. "He is very charming."

"Yes. But he is not a fit companion for a young girl learning her way about society."

"I thought he was a friend of yours?"

Why did the girl have to be so intelligent, Alicia wondered. She began to sympathize more with Ian. "He is a friend of my family, particularly one of my cousins," she answered. "I have known him since I was a child."

"And that makes a difference, I suppose." Marianne pondered. "Yes, I can see how it would. All right, I will take more care." She nodded once, decisively.

Alicia smiled. Marianne was very quick. "I'm sure you will find some of the younger men just as charming."

"Oh, I don't intend to keep away from Lord Devere," responded Marianne, as if that should be self-evident. "I shall simply be more on my guard with him. I did not realize that he had such a reputation. But I enjoy his company too much to give it up."

"But . . . there has been gossip." She was at a loss, and again felt younger than her years.

Marianne drew herself up, eyes flashing. "How odious people are! I thought they would be better here than at home."

Alicia remembered the story of the duel, and her uneasiness deepened.

"Well, I shan't pay any attention to it. *I* know I have done nothing wrong. That must be enough."

"But . . . gossip can do great harm." Alicia was amazed at her position. How often had she said precisely the same thing as Marianne, yet now she was taking the opposite side.

Marianne was again thoughtful. "Yes, I see. I *do*

wish to have a great success in town." She frowned. "But I will not become like those tongue-tied, awkward schoolgirls who huddle together at Almack's and giggle behind their hands."

"I don't think you could," replied Alicia, who had felt something similar herself once. She was very different from Marianne, she thought, and yet somehow like her, too.

The younger girl laughed. "No. Well, I thank you very much for your advice, Lady Alicia. I will not forget it."

Alicia felt that she should say more. Her purpose in coming was far from accomplished. But she could think of nothing. She rose.

Marianne did also. "It really was very good of you to come. Even if Ian urged you, I know you made up your own mind." She hesitated, then added, "I—I wish we might be friends, Lady Alicia."

Thinking back over their talk, Alicia found that their differences intrigued rather than put her off. "I hope we can," she answered warmly, holding out her hand.

Marianne squeezed it with a brilliant smile.

"Come and see me one day."

"I shall!"

With another exchange of smiles, Alicia took her leave. There was no sign of Cairnyllan, and she was glad of that. She felt happy, but she knew that if she had to report the results of her mission to him, he would spoil her buoyant mood. Thus, she hurried to her barouche and home, the smile lingering on her face.

The first person she encountered, in her front hall, was Roddy. He had been on the way out, but he turned back when she arrived. "There you are. I called to see if you would come driving in the park, and they told me you were out. Do you never stay home any more? This is the third time it has happened."

"Perhaps you should issue your invitations beforehand."

"I have! Twice. The first time you had forgotten, and the second you claimed to have the headache. I thought to catch you by surprise today." He gazed at her reproachfully.

Alicia had been feeling annoyed, but meeting Roddy's eyes, she found her irritation turning to guilt. She had treated him rather badly.

"You are so changed lately that I hardly know how to act," he added.

This decided her. She did not want to add to the gossip about her "strangeness." "Let me just speak to Lavinia, and we can go out."

"Truly?" Roddy smiled. "Splendid. I have my phaeton."

As she walked upstairs, Alicia again felt a twinge of guilt. She and Roddy had been friends for so long, and he had been so attentive to her wishes, that she often took his services for granted. Her recent experiences had given her a new sensitivity, however, and she decided that she must discourage Roddy from dangling after her any longer. It was little more than a game for her, and she had never before wondered whether Roddy felt the same. Now, she did, and determined to put an end to it.

When she had told Lavinia where she was going and adjusted her hat before the drawing room mirror, Alicia went back downstairs and was handed into Roddy's high-perch phaeton. He caught the thong of his whip jauntily as they set off for the park, and grinned at her in high spirits. "What have you been doing with yourself, Alicia? You never used to be so difficult to track down."

She shrugged. "I was making calls."

"Really? I thought you simply sat home and waited for us to come and worship at your feet." He grinned again, but Alicia did not smile. What a picture he presented. Seeing that she was not amused, he shifted his ground. "Have you heard the latest about Jane's and Willie's wedding? Her mother is insisting that it be put off three months, until some cousins or other return from abroad. Willie's in a fine temper, I can tell you. Last night at White's, he put his fist through a fellow's hat. Crusty old boy from the country, wouldn't you know. It was dashed awkward."

Alicia laughed. "Poor Willie. I must go and see Jane."

"*She* does nothing but cry, he says."

"I doubt it. And I doubt that the wedding will be put off. Have you never seen Jane managing her father?"

Roddy considered. "Well, but it's her mother cutting up rough."

"She will listen to Mr. Sheridan, once he declares himself. No, I wager the date will remain fixed."

"How much?" responded Roddy eagerly.

"What?"

He flushed a little. "Beg pardon. Forgot myself. We were all laying bets at the club last night, and I . . ."

Alicia laughed again. "Despicable. Is there nothing you will not bet on, Roddy? One week it is a race between a goose and a pigeon, the next a friend's wedding day. You are all mad on the subject." Suddenly remembering her own involvement with gambling, she flushed and fell silent. But Roddy merely grinned and shrugged, using the turn into the park as an excuse to avoid answering.

They drove along the Row in silence for a while. "Not many people out as yet," commented Alicia.

"I *tried* to take you at the fashionable hour. Twice."

"It is nicer now. Less crowded." Alicia was a bit apologetic. She gazed at the riders and strollers on either side of them. Her glance passed over a couple on the right, then swung back to survey them more closely. "Look there. Isn't that Lady Cairnyllan with Sir Thomas Bentham?"

Roddy looked. "Yes. You've heard that story, of course?"

"About the two of them?" He nodded, and she smiled. "I knew it. She broke his heart years ago, didn't she?"

"On the contrary. He broke hers."

"What?"

"You mean you really haven't heard? You always know all the gossip."

"Tell me," commanded Alicia.

"Well, I had it from Oswald, who got it from his great aunt, so I don't vouch for——"

"Roddy!"

"Yes, very well. It seems that Sir Thomas was Lady Cairnyllan's chief suitor. Before she married, I mean. Forget her name then. Everyone was expecting an announcement in the *Morning Post* when he suddenly joined up and went off to the war in America. Some talk of adventure and seeing the world before he settled down, they say. A few weeks later, Lady Cairnyllan—or whatever her name was—became engaged to Cairnyllan. They were married and in Scotland—she was anyway—before Sir Thomas returned. They never met again."

"Until now," added Alicia.

"Right." Roddy glanced at the pair again. "Seem to be picking up where they left off, eh?"

"She married in a fit of pique," murmured Alicia. "I daresay she was sorry at once."

"From what I've heard of Cairnyllan, she ought to have been," replied Roddy bluntly. "Was, in fact. Do you suppose she'll get Bentham this time? He's being dashed attentive."

"Oh, don't be vulgar, Roddy!" He stared at her. Alicia, half surprised at her own reaction, looked away. "It is such a romantic story. Why spoil it?"

Roddy continued to stare. He was finding the girl he thought he knew quite incomprehensible. "Are you going missish on me, Alicia? You've never talked such rubbish in your life."

He was right, she knew. In the past, she would have laughed with him at the revival of love in middle age, and assessed the chances of a renewed match. But somehow, after talking with Lady Cairnyllan at Vauxhall, she felt protective of her. And a flood of gossip might well wither the budding romance if Sir Thomas heard it. He was known to be a very proud man. Alicia shook her head at her thoughts. What had happened to her? All her feelings seemed oversensitized. She followed her familiar routine, but it now seemed peopled with new creatures both more complicated and more vulnerable than before. *Was* she growing missish? Or had she been somehow blind before? The thought made her shiver.

"Cold?" wondered Roddy. It was a balmy day, and Alicia wore a pelisse.

"No. Oh look, there is Emma. Pull up beside her."

He did so, and they were at once diverted into

discussing Jane's and Willie's wedding plans once again. Emma had just come from the Sheridans' and had new information. Alicia gratefully subsided into silence, leaving Roddy to engage in a spirited exchange about Jane's fortitude, which Emma stoutly defended. The world had not suddenly changed, Alicia mused. This conversation might have taken place last Season, or the one before. It must be she who was altered. And only one person could be responsible: Ian MacClain. She felt a flash of hot resentment. He had swept into her life, rejected her with contempt, and now apparently transformed her in some mysterious way. It was intolerable! Why had she insisted upon helping him with his sister?

But this brought back thoughts of her talk with Marianne, and with Lady Cairnyllan earlier. It had nothing whatsoever to do with *him,* she concluded. She was merely making amends for a mistake that might harm a charming girl who had done nothing to her. Lord Cairnyllan didn't matter a snap of her fingers.

"Alicia. I say, Alicia," complained Roddy.

She started. "What?"

"Don't you think so?"

"Think . . . about what?"

Roddy and Emma exchanged speaking glances, and Alicia couldn't help flushing slightly. "I was wondering about the time," she responded lamely.

"Well, I hope we're not keeping you from something *really* amusing," replied Roddy, stung.

"No, I didn't mean . . . that is . . ." Alicia stopped. She had never been clumsy in her life. What had come over her?

"Don't you think Jane will win out?" put in Emma,

moved by her friend's discomfort. "I say she will, but Roddy will not believe me."

Alicia nodded. "She will."

"See!" Emma was triumphant. "You simply don't understand a woman's methods, Roddy."

"No, I don't!" he answered, but he was watching Alicia.

Nine

"Lord Trehune called while you were out yesterday," said Lavinia at breakfast. "He was very eager to talk to you." She was not surprised at Alicia's disinterested nod, knowing the history of his unsuccessful courtship. "I shall go out this morning to buy some lengths for sheets," she added. Alicia's response was the same, again predictably. But Lavinia had been saving her best gleanings for last. "I spoke to Colonel Parker last evening. He saw your father in Vienna not two weeks ago and reports he is in fine spirits."

"That's good," answered Alicia absently.

Lavinia stared. She was accustomed to her cousin's boredom with domestic details and rejected suitors, but news of the duke had always captured her attention in the past. She eyed her more closely. Alicia had a peculiar vacant look in her pale blue eyes, and, though she was as lovely as ever, there was a novel hint of carelessness in her dress. Her sprigged muslin morning gown was perfect, but the usual little touches to complete her toilette were absent. "I am thinking of dismissing Cook," ventured Lavinia.

"Um," was the only response.

Lavinia's eyebrows came together. The Morland cook was universally acknowledged to be a treasure. Several hostesses had tried to lure her away, but she had been with the family nearly all her life and was staunchly loyal. Lavinia would no more think of dismissing her than Alicia would imagine letting her. "The house is on fire," said Lavinia in a cheerful tone. "And the head groom sent to say that all your carriage horses are down with grippe."

"Whatever you think best, Lavinia," murmured her companion.

Another woman would have asked her what was the matter, but Lavinia had developed more subtle ways of dealing with Alicia during the uneasy early days of their association. Alicia refused to be questioned or dictated to, but she could sometimes be made to believe that certain schemes or changes of plan were her own idea. Lavinia had learned to use her considerable intelligence and powers of observation first, then to guide unobtrusively.

Alicia's continuing strangeness was beginning to concern her. She was not ill, and Lavinia knew of no problem that should make her so different. She had made discreet inquiries among her friends, and found only a mirror of her own mystification. She had one or two thoughts, and now, she felt, the time had come to test them. "Was your drive in the park pleasant?" she began.

Alicia nodded again.

"Roderick was so pleased to catch you. Where had you been calling? I couldn't remember to tell him."

"I went to see Lady Marianne MacClain."

"Oh yes. She is a pleasant girl?" Lavinia watched her charge closely, for she had never known her to so distinguish a younger girl.

"She is," answered Alicia, showing more animation. "Quite unusual, really. I asked her to visit, so you will be seeing her again."

"Ah, good." Lavinia calculated, then said, "I have heard the talk about her father. Does Lady Marianne feel it too deeply?"

Alicia laughed. "Oh no. I don't think she cares a whit."

"I suppose she is too young to understand." Lavinia gauged the other's smile. "The mother and brother are more affected, perhaps."

Alicia's lips turned down. "No doubt."

Feeling that she was closing on her prey, Lavinia added, "Lord Cairnyllan is a fine figure of a man."

"I really hadn't noticed," replied Alicia coldly. She rose. "I must go and get my hat. I am to see the dressmaker at ten."

"Of course. We will meet at luncheon."

Alicia swept out, and Lavinia put her chin in her hand. She could scarcely believe it, but all the evidence pointed to the event she had waited and wished for for so long. She had come to Alicia far too late to teach her very much or change her habits. Only one thing, she had long ago concluded, would soften the girl's imperious manner and leaven her fine but slightly selfish character with a dash of humility. Alicia must fall genuinely in love. Lavinia had confidently expected it for years, and been repeatedly disappointed. Now, she was nearly certain the thing had happened. And Alicia was reacting just as she had known she would. Lavinia smiled as she left the breakfast table, and vowed to redouble her observations of a certain Scottish gentleman.

They would make a handsome pair, she thought as she went upstairs. And naturally he would worship Alicia, as what young man did not. It would be such a pleasure to see her charge happily settled, and to return herself to her peaceful former life.

When she entered her bedchamber to fetch her hat and gloves, she answered the chorus of eager greetings with a laugh. "Yes, Bess, Alfred, Boadicca. We will soon go home again, and you will see all your friends we had to leave behind." She bent to stroke the spaniels' long silky ears, and they romped around her uttering short, sharp barks. "Yes, yes. Harold is there, and Egbert and William Rufus. How happy they will be to see you. And you will have your own house again, just as you used. Do you remember?" Lavinia recalled her extensive kennels with a sigh. She had once been known as one of the foremost breeders of King Charles spaniels, but her stay in London had ended that. Perhaps this time next year, she would be back to it. With a renewed smile, Lavinia reached for her bonnet.

One of the chief events of the Season was to take place that night, a ball given by the Duchess of Rutland. When Alicia and Lavinia met for dinner before hand, the latter was much more pleased with the results of her day. In the course of a series of errands, Lavinia had spoken with a number of Alicia's friends and acquaintances, and without revealing anything herself, she had picked up a great deal of information. She was now practically certain of her theory, and she had dressed for the ball in a happy haze of anticipation, chattering to her dogs of their fast-approaching departure and contentedly contemplating her cousin's happiness.

Alicia responded laconically to her chaperone's bright flow of conversation. Her day had been wearisome, and she did not expect any particular pleasure from the ball. The dissatisfied expression on her face was at odds with her appearance, for she looked even more beautiful than usual. Alicia seldom wore white;

she had not favored it even when first out, and she now felt she was beyond the age of unrelieved pastels. But tonight she had, on impulse, put on a ballgown of pure white, its severe lines unmarked by any trim. It was a dress so simple and unassuming that no one could mistake it for other than the product of the best modiste in London. With it she wore white slippers and one silver bracelet. Around her neck was a narrow white ribbon, supporting a finely etched cameo. The lack of color made the blue of her eyes and the red of her lips and cheeks the more striking, and her silver blond hair seemed to scintillate in the candlelight.

But when Lavinia complimented her on her looks, she merely shrugged, and she said almost nothing through dinner and the short carriage ride to the Duchess's townhouse.

The ballroom was already full when they walked in. Not even the most haughty of the *haut ton* had refused this invitation, and from all sides could be heard languid complaints about the shocking squeeze, delivered in such complacent accents as to broadcast the speaker's true sentiments. Alicia and Lavinia made their way to a group of friends, but a few moments later the dancing began and Alicia was led away.

The first three sets passed in familiar conversation with partners she had danced with since childhood. But then the orchestra struck up a waltz, and Alicia was confronted by Lord Cairnyllan. "May I have the honor?" He bowed slightly before her.

Without thinking, Alicia gave him her hand, and they joined the dancers, Lavinia smiling happily behind them.

They moved in silence for several moments. Alicia

was wondering why she had come with him unhesitatingly, when she had vowed to avoid the man, and Cairnyllan was marveling at the woman in his arms. When Alicia had come in tonight, he had almost gasped aloud at her luminous beauty. All in white, she had seemed the embodiment of feminine loveliness and purity, and he again found it hard to reconcile what he knew of her with this image. He had been drawn irresistibly to her, and had tried three times to capture her attention. But each time another was quicker, and he had been forced to watch her on the dance floor with a London "dandy." When the waltz began, he was waiting and slipped in at once. Now, so close to her that her mild scent was dizzying, he could think of nothing to say. He didn't want to converse. He wanted to abolish even the narrow distance that separated them by crushing her against him. But the pause was growing awkward. "You visited Marianne, I believe?" he said, and was surprised to hear the coolness of his own voice.

Alicia had been dreading this question. "Yes."

She sounded even cooler, he thought, and a spark of quick resentment flared. Why should his mind and his body be in such opposition? This woman had no right to appear so wholly one thing and to be so much another. "I assumed you would keep me informed of your progress," he added coldly.

Alicia wished herself elsewhere. "Progress?"

"We agreed, did we not, on a *temporary* alliance to separate my sister from Lord Devere?"

Alicia wondered how it was that Cairnyllan had only to speak to enrage her. The tone in which he said "temporary" made her want to hit him. He sounded as if she were an annoyance rather than a voluntary helper. "After having talked with her, I'm not certain we should interfere," she answered. She had not meant to tell him her true opinion; she knew he would disagree violently, and she was not sure enough of it to make a defense. But as usual, she forgot her calm resolves in his presence.

"I see. And how, pray, did Marianne win you over?"

"She is a very sensible girl!"

"My sister? Say rather that you are easily gulled."

Alicia's blue eyes flashed. "Does it ever occur to you, Lord Cairnyllan, for even an instant, that someone else might judge better than *you* on certain questions?"

"Naturally, it does! But in the case of my own sister and an unknown Londoner whose standards I know to be lax, I believe I can safely——"

"You pompous, self-satisfied . . . stick!" Alicia was so angry she could hardly speak; she nearly pulled away from him then and there. But the satisfaction of deserting him in the middle of the dance floor would be dissipated by the uproar it would cause. "If you say another word, I shall scream. And I withdraw my offer to help you. Do precisely as you wish. I shall be the first to laugh when you make a fool of yourself before everyone." She would become Marianne's friend, she thought, and try to advise her if she needed it, but she would not spend another instant with her odious brother.

"I'm sure you will," he responded. "It is one of your chief amusements here in town. But as I shall know I am not a fool, it won't signify."

"I hope your sister *marries* Devere! It would be only your just deserts. And I hope your mother *elopes* with

Sir Thomas." Alicia's temper had gotten the best of her, and she was saying whatever came into her head.

"Do not drag my mother's name into this!" Cairnyllan's eyes blazed so that Alicia almost quailed. "It is obvious that you know nothing of her sort of woman. If you did, you could not have formed such an idea, let alone uttered it." Cairnyllan's hand had clenched so tight that Alicia had to protest. He released it, but his rage did not abate. From his earliest years, he had idolized his mother. Watching her endure the insults and neglect of his profligate father, he had come to see her as the epitome of pure, long-suffering womanhood. In all those years, he thought, hardly a complaint or reproach. She was above the sordid concerns that obsessed the *ton*. If only he could find another such, he would be content. But he would not find her here; that was obvious. Cairnyllan was completely unaware that a good part of his rage was at this exclusion of Alicia.

Alicia felt slightly repentant. She should not have mentioned elopements. But when Lady Cairnyllan was waltzing with Sir Thomas, in plain view, and nestled very close to him at that, it seemed a bit thick to claim she knew nothing of such feelings. Her expression mutinous, Alicia followed the couple with her eyes.

Cairnyllan, gazing down at her resentfully, glanced in the same direction. At that moment, Sir Thomas bent his head and murmured something in Lady Cairnyllan's ear. She laughed, shook her head, and tapped him playfully on the shoulder with her folded fan.

Alicia looked up, saw the direction of her partner's regard, and suppressed a smile. Really, it was ridiculous. When Cairnyllan made a strangled sound in his throat, she couldn't help but laugh a little.

He glared at her, unable to speak. It seemed to Ian MacClain that his whole world was turning topsy-turvy.

To Alicia's profound relief, the music ended. She slipped away at once and rejoined Lavinia, refusing to care that Cairnyllan remained stock-still where she had left him, his expression stricken.

"Did you enjoy the dance, dear?" asked Lavinia, with a secret smile.

"Hardly. Lord Cairnyllan is a boor." But she kept her eyes on him, missing Lavinia's abrupt change of expression. He had recovered, she saw with a twinge of relief, and was walking away. She hoped he had learned a lesson.

Roddy came up and claimed her for the country dance, and she went, losing sight of Cairnyllan and never noticing Lavinia's chagrin.

Alicia spoke no more to Cairnyllan that evening. He did not leave—she glimpsed him once or twice as the ball went on—but he stayed on the sidelines, observing, and did not dance again. She made a point of showing her enjoyment, laughing gaily at the least excuse and tossing back her silver-blond hair. But after supper, she grew rather tired of the charade, and at last she refused a dance and went to sit by Lavinia. As she did so, she noticed Marianne joining the set on Devere's arm. It was another waltz. She should speak to her, Alicia thought, to both of them, and she resolved to catch the pair when the music ended.

Thus, when Marianne and Devere went in search of refreshment a bit later, Alicia was ready. She joined them as he handed the girl a glass of lemonade.

"Lud, how I adore dancing," said Marianne. "Isn't this wonderful?" She was becomingly flushed and very lovely in a gold satin gown.

"You are the most wonderful thing about it," responded Devere. He nodded. "Alicia."

Alicia watched both of them. Robert seemed genuinely admiring, and Marianne full of confident high spirits. She did not appear overly impressed with Devere's manner or consequence.

"In Scotland, we had only a monthly assembly. In the summer! But here I have been to four balls already, in three weeks." Marianne smiled brilliantly at them both. "It is my idea of heaven."

"And your partners'," said the gentleman.

"What a plumper! You said you dislike debutante balls above all things."

"Not when I can dance with you," replied Devere.

Marianne laughed, and Alicia thought again that she seemed in little danger of losing her head. She did not blush or simper over Robert's compliments. Indeed, she seemed to take them with an amazingly sensible lightness. Where had she developed such assurance?

A young man came up and reminded Marianne of a promise to dance. She laughed again, handed Devere her now empty glass, and went off on the young man's arm. Devere eyed the container ruefully, one eyebrow raised, before signaling a servant and passing it on.

"Met your match, Robert?" asked Alicia, then immediately wished she hadn't. She did not want to put him even more on his mettle.

But he seemed merely thoughtful. "I don't know. It

is a possibility, however, and I have never been inclined to say that before. Fascinating."

Alicia searched for some discouraging remark. "Aren't you feeling rather bored with schoolgirl raptures?"

"Do you know, I am not. It is the oddest thing. I think it is because her enjoyment is so genuine, and so deep. It is a pleasure to watch her plunge her whole soul into a dance or a new sort of fruit ice. She has such . . . gusto."

This was far more serious than Alicia had imagined. She had never seen Robert in this mood. Clearly, he would not be persuaded to abandon Marianne just now. What if he actually offered for her, thought Alicia? It would be the coup of the season. Could Marianne resist accepting? And should she refuse? Robert would make a fine husband where he truly loved; she had always thought so. But Ian MacClain was unlikely to agree. What if her unthinking predictions of a moment ago came true? Not the elopement, of course, but the two matches. With his mother and sister married to Londoners, wouldn't the Earl of Cairnyllan have to change his opinions? Alicia started to smile at the picture, but for some reason her amusement was overridden by pity. He would be left quite alone, in a rather wrenching way. She bit her lower lip.

"Worried, Alicia?" wondered Devere. "Your concern for Lady Marianne's safety is beginning to seem superfluous. Perhaps you should fear for mine."

"Perhaps I was."

His hazel eyes flickered, and his smile wavered. But he recovered at once and laughed. "It has not come to that yet, my dear."

"Indeed?" She could not resist teasing him. It was

so novel to see Robert in the position where he had put so many of her sex.

"Indeed not. But I am deplorably forgetful. Will you dance?"

"Why not?" She took his proffered arm.

"Your eagerness overwhelms me," he murmured, and she laughed.

Alicia enjoyed the dance. In spite of everything, she found Robert very amusing and, with her worry over Marianne allayed, she could again appreciate his caustic wit. When they parted, she danced with another friend, and the remaining sets passed in the same way. It did not seem long before Lavinia came to suggest they call for the carriage. But the crowd was indeed thinning, and Alicia went upstairs to fetch her wrap.

As she was coming out of the ladies' retiring room, she heard voices from the stairs and paused, recognizing them.

"But you must remember," Sir Thomas Bentham was urging. "It was the night of the Duchess of Devonshire's Venetian gala. You can't have forgotten the gondolas. We rode together, remember. And you were cold. It was just after that that I gave you the roses."

"I really can't recall," answered Lady Cairnyllan.

Alicia stood stock-still, astonished by the tones of their voices. She had conversed with Sir Thomas on a number of occasions and certainly never heard him use those soft, caressing tones. And she would have sworn that the meek Lady Cairnyllan was incapable of that flirtatious, teasing riposte. It was a revelation —they were so old!—and yet somehow touching and cheering as well.

They had continued walking upstairs as they spoke,

and now they encountered Alicia at the top. She smiled and greeted them, amused to see both her elders look self-conscious and even slightly guilty. She didn't stay to embarrass them further, but passed by and down to Lavinia. Yet, throughout the drive home she had to restrain herself from fits of giggling.

Ten

Alicia had just sat down to write a letter to her father the following morning when a caller was announced. She abandoned her pen with a sigh. It was very odd, but although she was going out less often than usual, she seemed to have an even shorter time for correspondence.

Emma swept into the drawing room looking reproachful. "Here I am again, you see. You have not come to me, so I am forced to plague you with repeated visits."

"You could not plague me, Emma," replied Alicia with a smile. She indicated the sofa, and they sat down.

"Well, I hope not. But you haven't called, Alicia, and you promised you would. Last Season you did not neglect me."

"I have been remiss in all my calls, Emma. Forgive me." It was true, thought Alicia as she said it. She didn't know quite where the time was going, but many of her familiar duties had not been done lately.

"You called on that Scottish girl," Emma retorted. "You have leisure for *her*, but not for old friends."

Alicia stared at her. Neither the comment nor the petulant tone was at all like the light-hearted Emma.

Seeing her expression, Emma shook her head and looked down. "I beg pardon, Alicia. I am not feeling quite the thing these days. I—I am going to present Winthrop with an heir, and . . . it is the oddest sensation." She had flushed slightly, and now she raised her eyes as if nervous of Alicia's reaction.

"Emma! My congratulations. But you are happy about it, aren't you?"

Her friend's flush deepened. "Oh yes. And Jack is positively bursting." She grimaced. "If you had seen the letter he wrote his mother . . ."

Alicia laughed. "Well, then?"

"It is just, as I said, it is an odd sensation. I . . . I suppose I am a little frightened." Emma bit her lower lip and gazed at her.

"But your mother will help. And Jack's."

"I know, I know. It is nothing. Just . . . I have the strangest fancies sometimes. I seem different to myself." Impulsively, she reached out a hand and took Alicia's. "You *will* be my friend, won't you, Alicia? You won't drop away and leave me with the dowagers?"

"Of course I will! And of course I will not." Alicia laughed, squeezing the other's hand. "Dowagers indeed. Emma!"

Emma laughed a little also, embarrassed, and they fell silent. Alicia thought that, whatever their intentions, they *were* drawing apart. Lately, things had been slowly changing between them. Emma had new duties and responsibilities. And now . . . how odd it was to think of her as a parent. It made Alicia at once a bit sad and very interested and excited. She was surprised to discover a twinge of envy as well. Emma was moving into realms where she could not follow— she, who had always been the leader. And they would never be simply two carefree girls again. "You will adore him when he arrives, wait and see," she said stoutly.

Emma sighed. "Oh, I know I shall. I am being silly." She smiled. "It is well you say 'he.' Jack will have an apoplexy if it is not."

"Of course it will be a boy." Alicia's blue eyes twinkled. "Or if it is not, I'm certain Jack will come round."

"But his mother!" They both giggled.

"And only think of the shopping you must do," added Alicia. This time they laughed. Emma's love of shopping was proverbial.

"I have begun already. I saw the most cunning silver cup at—"

But she was interrupted by the announcement of another caller, and fell silent disappointedly.

"Am I interrupting you?" asked Marianne MacClain from the doorway, intercepting Emma's resentful gaze. "You said I might visit, Lady Alicia, but if I have chosen an awkward time, I . . ."

Thinking that really she had, Alicia rose and denied it. "We were just chatting. Come and sit down. Have you met my dear friend Emma, Lady Winthrop?"

The two expressed ignorance of each other, and Alicia performed the introductions. But a pall had fallen over the drawing room which her several attempts at conversation seemed unable to lift. Emma looked sulky and Marianne bewildered and uncomfortable. Alicia did not feel justified in returning to their former topic without some sign from her friend, and so was limited to banalities.

At last, her annoyance obvious, Emma rose. "I should go, I suppose."

Alicia also stood, relieved. She did not want to hurry Emma away, but it was clear that the three of them could not be comfortable.

But Marianne sprang to her feet as well. "No, don't you go. *I* shall. I broke in on your talk, and I am very sorry."

Emma blinked. This was a most unusual response. A conventional deb, in such an awkward situation, would have silently allowed her to depart, and then perhaps gossiped about her when she was well away. She looked at Marianne more closely. The girl seemed perfectly sincere; she was actually turning toward the door.

Alicia hesitated. It might be best if Marianne called another time, but she did not wish her to feel unwelcome. It was unfortunate that Emma should be in this strange mood just now.

"Wait," said Emma at that moment. "Don't go. I beg your pardon." Marianne turned back. "I am in a peculiar state this morning, that's all. Let us sit down again." She and Alicia did so, and Marianne followed a moment later.

"Are you going to have a baby?" she asked then.

Alicia and Emma both gaped at her.

"Oh, I beg your pardon. My wretched tongue! It is just that you looked as if you were, and then you said . . . But it is none of my affair, *of course*. Only I am so fond . . . You are *married,* aren't you?" Her eyes grew round, and she blushed scarlet at her own temerity.

Emma laughed aloud and nodded, exchanging an amazed glance with Alicia. "But how did you know?" She looked down at her still slender figure, then up at Marianne.

The other girl's flush, impossibly, deepened. Her

face was almost the color of her hair by this time. "Please forget what I said. It just . . . slipped out. I was so sorry I had come, and you looked . . . Oh, I *wish* I could learn to mind my tongue. Most of the time I am all right, you know, and so my guard is down. Then, something *shocking* pops into my head, and before I know it, it comes out of my mouth as well." She sighed deeply. "It is all from growing up at the ends of the earth. If I had had someone to talk to besides Ian and the crofters. But . . ." She hung her head. "I used to run away and follow the midwife about. She didn't see anything wrong with it, but Mama and Ian . . ." She shook her head. "I learned the *look*, though."

"The 'look'?" responded Emma.

"Yes. When a woman is . . . you know." Her forthrightness had departed with her composure.

"And I have it?" Emma seemed pleased as much as surprised. Her brown eyes held a soft glow.

Marianne nodded, her lips pressed together as if to prevent further revelations.

"How very odd." Emma's gaze strayed to the mirror over the mantel. Alicia and Marianne watched her with curiosity and respect. "You really are an extraordinary girl, aren't you?" she concluded finally.

Marianne grimaced. "People usually use a harsher word. Particularly my brother."

"Did you really visit the village midwife as a child?" wondered Alicia.

"I spent many of my days with her when I was small. My childhood was . . . irregular. Papa was most often away, you know, and Ian had to support Mama's spirits during . . . but never mind that. Are you sure you don't wish me to go?"

The older girls exchanged a glance and protested as one. Alicia in particular felt a renewed sympathy for Marianne, and for her brother as well. She had sometimes regretted things about her own youth—the early death of her mother and constant absences of her father—but she realized now that there had been nothing truly harsh about it. She had been surrounded by loving aunts and uncles and a host of boisterous cousins whom she led in fantastic pranks. Compared with the glimpse of her life Marianne had provided, she had been blessed. "Did you enjoy the ball last night?" she asked, knowing this for a safe subject.

"Oh yes!" Marianne's despondence vanished, and the three girls plunged into an animated discussion of recent entertainments. Before the visit ended, Emma was inviting Marianne to call on her, and they had agreed to a mutual shopping expedition the following afternoon. Marianne had by no means exhausted the delights of the London shops, and, when Emma promised to show her a number of new ones, her eyes positively glittered.

Alicia saw them out with a smile, then returned to finish her letter before luncheon. She was just sealing the page when the butler came in to announce another visitor. "William has arrived from Morlinden, Lady Alicia. He says you will wish to see him."

"Yes indeed." She put the sealing wax aside, leaving the letter open for an addition. "Send him up here, Bates."

A few moments later, one of the chief grooms of the Morland riding stables came into the drawing room. A small, gnarled man of about sixty, he looked out of place and uncomfortable in the elegant city apartment, yet his unease was clearly that of a countryman in the city rather than any personal embarrassment.

"William, hello." Alicia smiled warmly at him.

"Your ladyship." He dipped his head.

"You've brought the youngsters up to Tattersall's?"

He nodded. "We've a good crop, though we kept the likeliest for ourselves, o' course. Will you be comin' down to see 'em, your ladyship?"

"Yes, we can go this afternoon. Did you bring Lightfoot? Or does he stay?" She tried to appear nonchalant.

William grinned. He had known Alicia since she mounted her first pony at three and promptly fell off when she tried to put him at a hedge nearly a foot taller than himself. And he had taught her a good bit of what she knew about horses, which would have been impressive in a man. "He stayed. A likely looking colt, Mr. Jenkins says."

Alicia laughed. "I told you so. He is sound as my Whitefoot. You thought he was short of wind."

"We watched him closer after you spoke," replied William. "And you was right." They exchanged a warm look, William proud of his former pupil and Alicia pleased with her expertise.

"Go and have something to eat," she told him, "and we will go out early in the afternoon."

"Very well, your ladyship." With another dip of his head, he went out.

They drove to Tattersall's in the early afternoon. The sale involving the Morlinden horses, and others, would be held the following day, and Alicia meant only to look over the animals William had brought. She never attended the sales themselves, though one or two women occasionally did. They went directly to the stables attached to the auction house, and William escorted her to those where his charges had been installed.

He had brought a total of ten horses, colts and fillies not considered quite up to Morlinden standards, though superior to many others. Alicia went from box to box looking them over and commenting on the choices. She found nothing to object to; William and the chief trainer, James Jenkins, were skilled. But she did occasionally regret the loss of a horse she had particularly noticed at birth.

"It's like children, ain't it, your ladyship?" said William at one point. "You watch them kind of hopeful like, and sometimes you're pleased and sometimes you're disappointed, but there ain't nothing you can do."

Alicia smiled at this comparison, but answered only, "I *am* disappointed to see Black Lady go. I was certain she'd be a winner."

William shook his head. "Mean tempered. We've done what we can, but she won't be taught. Bites something fearful, she does."

As they passed on to the next box and William stepped forward to open it for her, there was a sudden loud clatter, and a boy of about fourteen tumbled out to land in a huddle at their feet. Startled, Alicia moved back.

"Bob Rollins, you clumsy oaf!" exclaimed William. "What have you been up to now?"

The boy scrambled to his feet. He was as tall as William, but extremely lanky. His hands seemed too large for his body, and his brown eyes were frightened. With another smile, Alicia saw that an oak bucket was affixed to his right foot.

"If you've hurt that horse . . ." began William.

"I ain't. I tripped is all."

"Tripped. Or fell. Or knocked something. Can't you stay on your own feet for an hour when I let you do the watering?" William turned to Alicia. "Bob is the most ham-handed stableboy in the county. He's nigh to killed himself with every tool we've got. Trips over his own bootlaces." Bob, who had been surreptitiously trying to remove the bucket stuck on his boot, cringed slightly.

"Do you dislike working in the stables?" inquired Alicia, still smiling. "We might find a place for you . . ."

"Oh no, ma'am!" the boy broke in passionately.

"No, your ladyship," corrected William, adding grudgingly, "he do have a feeling for horses. He's never hurt one of them."

"I'll be more careful, your ladyship," pleaded Bob. "Don't go and send me away."

"Of course not, if you are happy."

Bob grinned all across his face. "Thankee." Seeing William's scowl, he quickly added, "Your ladyship."

"Well, go on with you then," said William, his eyes belying his harsh tone. "Take the bucket off your foot and be about your work, you great noddy."

Half bowing, half crouching to the bucket, Bob obeyed. He still had no success in dislodging it, so he limped hurriedly in the direction of the smith.

When he was gone, Alicia let go the laugh she had been restraining. Even William smiled, and they were both surprised by a deep masculine laugh behind them. Turning, Alicia confronted Ian MacClain, who said, "That young man will go far," his voice shaking with amusement.

Alicia's smile, which had begun to fade, returned.

"You handled him well," he added.

"I did nothing."

"Exactly." Ian eyed her approvingly. This glimpse of her among her stablemen had affected him very favorably. She seemed a different person from the glittering drawing room creature he deplored.

"Have you come to look over the horses before the auction?"

"Yes. You also?"

"In a manner of speaking. We are selling some stock from Morlinden, so William brought me over to see them."

Cairnyllan nodded to William. "What a lucky chance. Perhaps he has the time to show them to me as well? I should very much like to purchase the more promising of Royal Sir's line. I had not hoped to get expert information."

Alicia was slightly stung. "You think I could not show you myself? I know the horses quite as well as William." If this was not absolutely true, she thought a bit guiltily, at least she knew more than enough for *his* purposes.

"I merely assumed you were going soon," he replied.

"On the contrary, I have only just begun my inspection." Alicia's expression was haughty, but she was wondering why she had said such an idiotic thing. She was at the last box in the row, and *would* have departed in another few minutes. Moreover, Cairnyllan might have seen her looking at the other horses. She had no idea how long he had been watching. But there was nothing for it now but to retrace her steps and pretend unconsciousness of the unsettling gleam in his blue eyes.

They went together into the box nearest. Cairnyllan was quite as knowledgeable as Alicia, and indeed as William. He asked searching questions as he ran his hands down the colt's legs and looked at his teeth. As they walked to the next box, Alicia thought that she had not seen him so at home since they had left Perdon Abbey. His large frame moved with grace and assurance here, as it never did in a London drawing room. His expression was more relaxed and his conversation immeasurably pleasanter. Indeed, they were talking almost like old friends, she realized. "This is Black Lady," she said as they reached another stall.

"Ah. She's a beauty." Before Alicia or William could speak, he had opened the door and stepped inside. "Aren't you? Yes. What a coat."

"Look out," warned Alicia then. "She bites."

"This lovely creature?" Cairnyllan moved closer, holding out his hand to the horse.

"She do, sir," said William. "We couldn't break her of it."

"Perhaps you didn't ask her nicely enough." Mac-Clain slowly extended his hand, murmuring softly all the while, and stroked the filly's nose. She tossed her head at first, but did not bite. Gradually, soothed by something in the man's tone or manner, she quieted, finally nuzzling at the front of his coat. "She's gentle as a lamb," he said. "I shall certainly buy this one."

Alicia and William exchanged a glance, the latter shrugging helplessly. "She bit Jem Ellis so that he had to have his arm sewn up." William glared at Cairnyllan. "And he spoke as nicely as anyone could!"

Cairnyllan laughed. "Well, the lady must simply have her own opinions, then." He beckoned to Alicia. "Come and see."

A little wary, Alicia entered the box. Black Lady watched her, but did not shy. When she tried to put her hand on the horse's nose, however, she bared her teeth at once, and Alicia quickly drew her hand back.

"Here now," said Cairnyllan, "none of that." The filly nuzzled him again, and he laughed.

Both Alicia and William were feeling resentful. They moved on toward the next stall without speaking, and Cairnyllan followed, grinning, after one final pat. He was wise enough not to mention Black Lady again soon.

When they had seen all the Morlinden horses, they stood for a moment in the stableyard. "May I escort you home?" offered Cairnyllan.

"William came with me." She hesitated.

"But I am sure he would rather remain here with his charges."

William agreed that this was true, and Alicia took Cairnyllan's arm to walk back to her barouche. When he had tied his mount on behind, they started off, and a curious awkwardness descended upon the carriage. In the stables, they had talked without constraint. But now, side by side in the elegant vehicle, this ease seemed to have dissipated. Alicia was very aware of the earl's shoulder against hers, and his pantaloon-clad leg near her own. Memories of their first meeting and wild gallop came back to her, driving conversational gambits right out of her head.

Had she known how similar were Cairnyllan's thoughts, she might have felt even more unsettled. He was recalling their headlong embrace with more charity than he had ever done. It seemed to him at that moment as if his reservations about Lady Alicia did not matter. She might not be the kind of woman he had planned to love, but she was an extraordinary one. And she could not help the fact that she had been reared in town and learned town ways. He saw the necessity for making allowances as he never would have before. With his guidance, he thought, she might become the perfect companion. Smiling slightly, Cairnyllan lost himself in a fantasy of continual passionate rendezvous amidst the heather.

"So you will buy Black Lady?" asked Alicia in a rather stiff tone. She felt that one of them must speak to break the rising tension.

"What?" Cairnyllan's pleasant dream collapsed, and he felt unreasonably annoyed. "Oh, yes. I certainly shall."

"You won her over amazingly."

"I am known for my skill with temperamental fillies," he answered rather smugly. "I imagine they sense a stronger will when they encounter one."

Alicia was unaccountably enraged. "Indeed? Perhaps they 'sense' that you would beat them soundly if they did not obey."

He stared at her. He had never beaten a horse in his life.

"You do not strike me as possessing much restraint. And I think your sister would agree!"

Cairnyllan's frown slowly gave way to an incredulous smile. He had to make a strong effort not to laugh aloud. "We were talking of *horses*, were we not?"

Alicia blushed scarlet, a thing she had not done for years, and turned abruptly away. The man was utterly crude, to twist her words in such a way. Let them pass the whole journey in silence; she would say no more!

The earl gazed at her averted profile, and continued to smile. He had already begun to consider Alicia in a different light. Now he wondered if he was perhaps involved in a contest he *could* understand, rather than stumbling blindly amid a set of Londonish rules and fripperies. If so, there was hope that he might someday understand Alicia Alston, as he had thought he never would. The idea filled him with such relief that he did not even notice the lack of conversation or care that Alicia's farewell was markedly cool.

Eleven

A week passed without incident. Alicia and Lavinia attended several functions without seeing any of the MacClains, and Alicia was beginning to feel some of her old boredom again when Roddy burst into her drawing room one morning very soon after breakfast, looking disheveled. He had not paused to let the butler announce him, and he did not waste time on greetings. "You must come with me right away," he said. "You have called there before."

Alicia stared at him. She had been settling down to the household accounts and was considerably startled by his abrupt appearance. "What? Whatever are you talking about, Roddy?"

"Haven't you *heard*?"

"Heard what? Do sit down. You are towering over me in the most ominous way. And straighten your neckcloth. It is under your ear."

"There's no time for that," he answered, jerking the cloth into place. "I cannot believe you haven't heard the gossip. Marianne MacClain has *refused* Devere!"

"What?"

Roddy nodded, satisfied with her reaction, and sat down on the edge of the sofa. "He actually offered for her, and she turned him down. That is the *on-dit*, at least. I want you to take me there now so that we can discover the truth of the matter. *And* the details." His eyes gleamed with anticipation. "What a story I shall have for the ball tonight."

Alicia was too astonished even to tease him about his avidity. "Are you sure, Roddy? It seems so . . ."

He nodded. "We all thought Devere immune. But I had the tale on very good authority. Of course, I shall not be *sure* until we call." He rose and gave her an admonitory glance.

"You cannot seriously expect me to take you there at this time of the morning? I am not that well acquainted with them myself."

"Nonsense! You have visited several times."

"Once, Roddy."

"We will think of a plausible story." He considered. "We were out for a stroll, and happened to pass by." She looked at him. "Well, something else then. Alicia, you can't refuse. Think of it. Devere!"

She did think of it, and had to admit that her own curiosity was roused. Knowing Marianne, she could almost believe that the girl would throw away the greatest catch in the *ton*, and all the status capturing him would imply. But she could not imagine that Robert Devere had actually proposed. For as long as she could remember, he had seemed oblivious to eligible young ladies.

Seeing her expression, Roddy urged, "We needn't stay long. And Lady Marianne will *wish* to have the true story known."

"Oh, Roddy." But Alicia was wavering.

"You may tell them it was all my idea, if you like. Say I am a dreadful gossip and dragged you there."

"You are!"

He looked offended. "I have a normal interest in my friends' activities, naturally."

Alicia laughed. "Very well. Let us go. I should not, but I admit I am burning with curiosity."

"That's the girl!" He strode toward the door and was only with difficulty persuaded that Alicia must have her bonnet and shawl.

The streets were empty of fashionables as they drove to the MacClain house. Indeed, Alicia began to have second thoughts about their visit when she saw only tradesmen and peddlers about. "Marianne may be still in bed," she said as they climbed the three steps to the door and Roddy plied the knocker. "I don't suppose she will see us." As she spoke, she was suddenly struck by the thought that Lord Cairnyllan might be the one to receive them. No doubt he always rose early, even in town. She hung back as she pictured the scene. She did not want to appear before him seeking food for gossip.

Fortunately, both Cairnyllan and his mother were denied. The earl was out, and Lady Cairnyllan not yet downstairs. But when Alicia asked for Marianne, the servant looked uncertain. "I will inquire, miss," he said.

A few moments later, he returned to usher them upstairs to the drawing room. Marianne rose with an impish smile when they came in. "Lady Alicia. And Lord Roderick. How kind of you to call."

One glance at her dancing eye decided Alicia on honesty. "It isn't kind at all. Roddy positively forced me to bring him at this ridiculous hour because he wants to interrogate you."

"Me?" Marianne was the picture of amazed innocence, but once again her eyes gave her away.

She seemed to be enjoying the sensation she had caused.

Roddy was not quite up to Alicia's bluntness. "Not at all. Just passing by, you know, and popped in for a moment."

"It is so invigorating to drive out in the early morning hours," said Marianne. "Ian always rides then. He insists it is the most healthful time."

Roddy goggled at her. "Er, yes, to be sure. I've often said the same myself."

"Oh, Roddy, you rarely rise before noon," responded Alicia.

Marianne laughed at the chagrined expression on his face, and after a moment, Alicia joined her. "Lady Marianne knows perfectly well why we are here," she added. "Anyone can see that. Indeed, you might have known she would; she isn't stupid."

"Well, but . . . that is, no need to . . ."

Marianne laughed again. "You want to know what happened, I suppose. I shouldn't say anything, you understand, if the whole had not been overheard."

Roddy looked crushed. "By whom?"

"Two of Mrs. Jennings's servants."

"Oh, that's all right then. Servants' gossip is slow to get around." He paused. "Or slower than I shall be, at any rate." The girls laughed again, and he looked up, puzzled, then embarrassed. "I say, I didn't mean . . ."

"We know what you meant," laughed Alicia. "But if the story is common knowledge, Lady Marianne . . ."

"Well, Lord Devere offered for me last night, and I told him that although I was *very* flattered and conscious of the honor, I didn't wish to marry just yet." When she noticed her audience staring, she added, "I am only eighteen, you know, and I haven't even had one whole Season."

"Yes, but, *Devere!*" gasped Roddy.

"Well, I know he is thought a great catch. And I find him vastly amusing. But he is nearly twenty years older than me, and I don't think we should suit."

Roddy seemed bereft of speech, but Alicia eyed the younger girl with considerable respect. This was a new view of Robert, and as she adjusted to it, she saw that it was extremely sensible. She would have felt the same herself, she realized, had there ever been any question of marriage between her and Devere. "You are extraordinary," she said.

Marianne flushed a little. "I know you must think it odd. Everyone will, I suppose. It is just that——"

"Not at all. I meant extraordinarily wise."

Roddy gaped first at Alicia, then at Marianne. "And you just refused him? Just like that? One of the most eligible bachelors in the *ton*? I mean, you didn't hesitate even for an instant?" He seemed to be trying to fix the scene in his mind.

"Yes. It was over in a moment. Lord Devere said he understood perfectly and that he hoped we might still be friends. And I said of course we should, and he went off. I believe he is planning a visit to the country." Once again, the sparkle in her eyes showed that she saw the humor in this sudden decision.

"I daresay," responded Roddy feelingly. "He must know what a storm of gossip this will set off." He rose, then looked uneasy. "I mustn't keep you. You'll be wanting to get on with your, er . . ."

"Oh, I haven't anything planned," said Marianne airily. "My whole morning is free."

Roddy shifted from foot to foot, and the girls laughed. "Oh go on, Roddy," said Alicia. "I'm sure you'll be the first with the news."

He opened his mouth to make an excuse, then

closed it and grinned. "Right. I'm off then. Are you coming, Alicia?"

"No, I shall stay a moment. You will have to walk, or find a cab."

He held up a hand to show that this was understood, bowed to both girls, and withdrew, the sound of his footsteps telling them that he practically bounded down the stairs.

Alicia shook her head. "What a rattle he is."

"But sweet," replied Marianne.

Alicia smiled, dismissing the subject. "You have caused a sensation, you know."

"Yes." Marianne dimpled. "But it wasn't entirely my fault. He needn't have *asked* me."

"But do you have any idea . . ."

"Yes, I do!" All amusement gone, Marianne leaned forward and spoke very earnestly. "I won't enjoy being stared at and talked of, you know. It is exciting to be singled out, but I should prefer not to be *quite* so . . ." She hesitated, as if searching for a word, then used Alicia's with a small grimace, ". . . extraordinary. I could not marry him, however."

"Could not marry whom?" asked a deep voice from the doorway.

Marianne jumped. "Oh, Ian, how you startled me!"

Alicia turned to see the earl leaning against the jamb. He was dressed for riding and still held a crop against his leg. He smiled at her, and she was taken aback by the intensity of his gaze.

"If there is some question of your marrying, I think I should hear of it," he added. "Which of the young sprigs have you disappointed?"

Marianne seemed both annoyed and uncertain. "What does it matter, since I *have* done so?"

Cairnyllan came farther into the room. "It matters because you are my responsibility. Who, Marianne?"

"Perhaps I shan't tell you!"

Each of them did just the thing most calculated to annoy the other, Alicia thought, though she was not sure their behavior was conscious. On impulse, she said, "Lady Marianne has refused Lord Devere."

Marianne frowned, then shrugged. Cairnyllan swung around to look at her, his red brows drawn together. It took him a moment to digest the information. "Devere? I thought he was a great catch."

"He was—is," agreed Alicia.

Cairnyllan turned to his sister. "And I thought you were besotted with him."

"That just shows how little you know of me, Ian. I told you he was simply amusing."

Cairnyllan seemed to be having great difficulty taking this in. He had bent every faculty toward protecting Marianne and separating her from Devere's pernicious influence, and now it appeared that all his efforts had been unnecessary. His whole conception of his sister's character was thrown in doubt. "I don't understand," he murmured.

"I didn't wish to marry him," replied Marianne, as if this were obvious. "He is years older, and I do not love him."

"But you declared you wanted to live in town, to have a great position, to . . ."

"Well, if I can find those things in someone I care for, I do. You should not take what I say when I am angry with you so seriously, Ian."

"I see." He was eyeing her as if he had never seen her before. "But what of Devere? How will he take a rebuff? Will he not seek some revenge? Perhaps even an abduction . . ."

"Oh, Ian!"

Alicia suppressed a smile. "I fear you have been reading too many romantic novels, Lord Cairnyllan. According to reports, Robert plans a sojourn in the country, quite alone. I daresay he wishes to avoid the gossip attendant on his failure."

"Ah."

There was a short silence. Alicia considered the brother and sister. "I have just been telling Lady Marianne how I approve of her decision, and her understanding in general. I think she has been very wise, don't you?"

"Wise?" He looked at Marianne as if he had never before connected this word with her. "Why, yes, I suppose she has."

"You 'suppose'?" Marianne laughed. "Admit it, Ian, there is nothing whatever for you to criticize in this case. You cannot even deplore my hastiness!"

"Indeed, I congratulate you. You have done very well."

Marianne blinked, clearly affected by the compliment, and her brother continued to gaze thoughtfully at her.

Only Alicia found suitable words. "You are more alike than you know," she said slowly. And when they both turned to stare at her, she added, "How often has one of you done anything the other *really* disapproved?"

"Ian kept me in Scotland!" protested Marianne.

"Until you reached the terrific age of eighteen," Alicia replied, smiling.

"Marianne is far too free in her manners," said Ian. "She encourages——"

"And yet she refused the greatest match in London."

The two young MacClains gazed at one another.

"Marianne, have you seen my red sunshade with the ivory handle?" asked Lady Cairnyllan, coming into the drawing room pulling on her gloves. "I've looked everywhere and I can't find it."

"I believe you sent it to be repaired, Mama. The clasp was not holding, remember?"

"Why, to be sure, I did. I don't know where my mind is these days." But she smiled as if she had a fairly clear notion. "Lady Alicia, hello. I did not notice you at first."

Alicia eyed Lady Cairnyllan with interest and some amusement. Her weeks in town had certainly altered the silent, retiring woman she had been at Perdon Abbey. Though self-absorbed, there was no sign of shyness about her. And her looks were greatly changed as well. She stood straighter, and her dark eyes sparkled in a face that looked ten years younger. She had refurbished her wardrobe—the cherry-colored morning dress she wore was the height of fashion—and had her brown hair cut and curled. No one would take her for the mother of these two tall redheads.

Cairnyllan was also watching her, but not with Alicia's approval. "Something has happened, Mother. Marianne has received an offer of marriage."

"Really, dear?" Lady Cairnyllan turned to her daughter, appearing mildly interested. "Do you think you wish to marry so soon?"

"I refused," replied the girl, smiling.

"Oh, that's all right then. You're so young yet." She finished working her fingers into her ivory kid gloves.

"It was Lord Devere, Mother," said Ian in a sharper tone, as if he found her reaction incomprehensible.

"Devere?" Lady Cairnyllan looked from one to the

146

other of them, smiling vaguely, her thoughts clearly elsewhere.

"I spoke to you about him," said Cairnyllan.

"Umm? Oh, yes, that attractive thirtyish man. You wouldn't have suited, Marianne."

"I know, Mama." Marianne was grinning by this time, and Alicia was having trouble with her own expression.

"I am going driving with Sir Thomas," added Lady Cairnyllan. "I expect I shall be back for luncheon. Or perhaps not." She smiled to herself. "You don't need me, do you?"

Marianne shook her head. "I mean to go to Hookham's to exchange my book, but I can take Annie with me."

"You should not go out alone," began Cairnyllan automatically.

"I shan't. I shall take Annie." Marianne's blue eyes twinkled. "And Mama is going out alone."

"No, dear," replied her mother absently, "I am going with Sir Thomas. Is that a carriage?" She went to the window and looked down. "Yes. Good-bye, children. Lady Alicia." Smiling still, she went out.

Cairnyllan stood very still, an arrested expression on his face, and Alicia could not resist saying, "Your mother seems to be enjoying London."

"Oh yes," answered Marianne. "In fact, I think she likes it better than either of us. Certainly better than Ian." Both girls glanced at him, but he didn't notice. He was obviously trying to assimilate a number of new ideas. Alicia and Marianne exchanged an amused look.

"Sir Thomas is very attentive," said Alicia. She was enjoying herself. Ian MacClain was always so certain he was right; it was a pleasure to see him dumbfounded. Perhaps if he admitted his mistake in one case . . . but she turned from this thought. She didn't really care what he believed.

"He is," agreed Marianne, obviously feeling some of the same emotions as Alicia. "I believe he is sorry for what he did years ago."

This made her brother raise his head. "Did? What are you talking about?" he snapped.

"Haven't you heard the story? Roddy told me." Marianne giggled. "He couldn't resist, though he knew it was not quite the thing to gossip about my own mother."

"What gossip?" Cairnyllan looked outraged, and disbelieving. ·

Her voice carefully expressionless, Marianne repeated the story of the long-ago romance, much as Alicia had heard it. Her brother's response was abrupt. "That's the most ridiculous thing I have ever heard!"

"But why, Ian? Mama was a young girl once, too. And she naturally . . ."

"I forbid you to say any more about it," he interrupted. And turning on his heel, he strode out of the room.

There was a short silence, then Marianne said, "Ian has always practically worshiped Mama. It comes from the way our father acted when he was small."

Alicia nodded sympathetically. She too had seen the look of confusion in the earl's eyes. It could not be easy to have your ideal image changed. She remembered suffering through certain similar occasions with her father, and they had been far less radical.

"I think London is proving a further education for all of us," added the other girl. "It's very strange."

"You, at least, are profiting," replied Alicia with a smile.

"Oh, I expected to; I'm not sure Ian *or* Mama is getting precisely what was anticipated."

"I would be willing to wager they are not."

The girls' eyes met, and they both giggled.

"Are you really going to Hookham's?" asked Alicia then. "I should be glad to go with you. They have a new novel I have been wanting."

"Splendid." Marianne jumped up. "I'll get my hat."

Twelve

Alicia was not surprised when Lord Cairnyllan sought her out as soon as he entered Mrs. Crestwood's ballroom that evening. She had been certain he would have more to say on the subject of his mother's past, and that, since she had been present when he learned the story, he would say it to her, among others. Coincidentally, a waltz was beginning, and he reached her just ahead of another young man, who looked disappointed. "Will you dance?" asked Cairnyllan.

Alicia didn't think of refusing. She was far too curious about his state of mind. They moved onto the floor and swung into the waltz. The movement diverted both of them from Lady Cairnyllan. Though Cairnyllan had been thinking of little else for the past day, he was now conscious of nothing but the feeling of Alicia in his arms. The top of her head came just to his chin, he realized; she was not a dab of a woman, as so many were, and he needn't feel a clumsy giant. She danced as if she had legs, and did not cling and hesitate in the way he detested. Her scent rose about them in a heady cloud. He was reminded of his earlier thoughts regarding Black Lady, and the nature of fillies, and a smile curved his lips. She was beautiful and spirited and obstinate, and with her so close, he could think of nothing but pulling her closer still, as he had done once.

His clasp tightened involuntarily. Feeling it, and seeing his smile, Alicia became even more aware of him. His palm was roughened; she could feel the callouses that came from hard riding and, presumably, work on his estate. She might have derided such a thing once, but it seemed somehow right for this man and not at all bumpkinish. The tightening of his arm had brought her eyes within three inches of his coat lapels, and the warm grip around her waist was pleasant. She ought to draw back, she knew; they were rather too near for propriety. But she didn't want to. The conviction she had felt on first knowing him—that here was an equal and her natural partner —recurred, as did a flash of memory from Perdon Abbey. That day had been like nothing else in her life before or since. But the recollection inevitably evoked the scenes that had followed as well, and Alicia's cheeks reddened slightly. She searched her mind for an innocuous remark, at the same time pulling a little away. "It is very hot, isn't it?" she managed. "I don't believe Mrs. Crestwood has opened even one window."

"Perhaps she is not as fond of fresh air as we are." His tone implied a host of meanings, and his blue eyes held hers for a moment.

Rightly interpreting this as a reference to their gallop, Alicia turned her head away. How dare he refer to it after the way he had treated her? But she found only the smallest spark of anger in her breast, and it was nearly stifled by a thrill of excitement. Annoyed by her own susceptibility, she pressed her lips together. "Did your mother and sister accompany you tonight?" she asked.

Her diversion was successful. Cairnyllan frowned and looked around the ballroom. "Yes." He saw Marianne dancing with an unexceptionable young man, and Lady Cairnyllan talking to some of the dowagers in the far corner. Relaxing a little, he added, "You should not take the gossip about my mother seriously, you know. Gossip is always exaggerated, and usually wrong."

"I don't know what you mean by 'take seriously.' I thought it a charming story."

Cairnyllan's frown deepened. "Your style of life has made you far too fond of scandal."

"And yours has made *you* completely misunderstand the meaning of that word," she retorted. "There is no 'scandal' in the story of your mother's and Sir Thomas's old romance. It is perfectly innocent. They were two young people who nearly married once; that is all."

"My mother is not a hardened flirt!"

Alicia looked up at him in exasperation. He really was *so* obtuse. "No one imagines that she is, or was," she replied. "I really cannot understand . . ."

"No, you cannot." He hesitated, then slowly added, "My mother is . . . like a child, you see. The difficulties of her life—her disappointments and isolation—failed to crush her, but they drove her to a kind of naiveté. I had to do everything for the family. She has no understanding of the sort of thing you mean." He sounded rather proud of this.

Alicia was unimpressed. "In the first place, it is not I who 'means' anything whatsoever. *I* didn't begin the gossip, and I have not repeated it. But I wonder whether it was good for your family for you to do 'everything'?"

"I beg your pardon?"

"Your mother and sister may have wished to do some things for themselves." She smiled slightly. "I know Marianne did, and it might have done your mother good to take charge."

"This is none of your affair," he answered coldly, his face closed.

"No. And it is quite off the subject as well. I was merely trying to point out to you that the story of Lady Cairnyllan and Sir Thomas was touching and innocent."

He did not look at her. "I wonder if you would feel the same if it were your mother?"

Alicia considered. It was a bit difficult to picture her lost mother, but she felt no distaste. As a further test, she imagined her father in the same position, then shook her head. Lord Cairnyllan was simply mistaken. Even when she thought of her father engaged in any number of desperate flirtations now—and as a handsome and eligible man of sixty, he might well be—she felt nothing more than amused condescension. Had he lived in London, of course, or been like the previous Lord Cairnyllan . . . this thought brought her up short, and she felt a flood of sympathy for her partner. It was no wonder he had distorted ideas about these things, having endured such a father. But it was time he saw the truth, before he hurt both his mother and himself. "Yes," she said positively, "I should feel just the same. I am certain my mother had suitors before my father appeared, and I'm sure he courted other girls as well. You see it happening all around us." She indicated the other dancers.

"This was rather more serious, and . . . Mother is not that sort of person." He eyed a laughing debutante with distaste.

"Is it because she was, in a manner of speaking, jilted?" said Alicia. "It is not——"

"Nothing of the sort! I do not care to discuss this subject any further." His face was set.

"But I was only——"

"It is hardly a proper topic for us in any case. Who is that young man dancing with Marianne?" Resolutely, he thrust the thought of his mother's romance away. It was wholly at odds with his image of her as a cloistered and martyred ideal to be protected and shielded by his care. That recent events had called that image into question, he refused to consider just now.

Alicia sighed and gave it up. There was no reasoning with the man. "That is Denniston. He is the son of the Duke of Selbridge. Very charming."

"Marianne seems quite taken with him." He frowned. "Why must she throw back her head and laugh so loudly? If she would only curb her natural enthusiasm a little . . ."

"Yes, she seems to be thoroughly enjoying herself. What a pity." Alicia's sarcasm was unmistakable.

"You think little of my morality, I know," responded Cairnyllan. "What you do not understand is that I am wholly responsible for——"

"Nonsense!" He stared at her. "You have convinced yourself that no one but you can look after your family, and that no one but you knows how they should go on. But your sister is an astonishingly sensible girl, who can judge for herself in almost any situation. Look at the way she handled Devere. And your mother seems well able to think for herself as well. Perhaps they are both weary of your 'morality.'"

For an instant, he looked stricken. Since his earliest youth, he had thought of little but his family, and how to support their spirits and position. Along with caring for the estate, this task had been his life. And now this fashionable Londoner was suggesting that he had been mistaken, or that his duties were over. "You are very ready to offer advice on matters that are none of your affair," he answered.

Alicia started to reply, then hesitated and smiled slightly. "I have often been told so," she agreed.

Her capitulation surprised him. "I know that Marianne is growing up," he temporized. "And soon she will marry. I shall be happy to see her settled with a suitable husband."

"Of your choosing?" Alicia was still smiling.

"Well, I should hope that I . . . that is, if she should consult . . ." He grimaced. "Damn you, no! I am not a petty tyrant. If Marianne will avoid choosing some entirely unacceptable . . ."

"As she recently did," put in Alicia.

"As she did," he agreed savagely. "Then, of course, I will be happy to welcome the man she does settle on."

"How generous!" Alicia grinned. "And since she has demonstrated her good sense, no doubt you mean to leave her to discover this paragon for herself."

Cairnyllan glared at her, then very slowly began to smile. "I suppose so."

"It will be terribly difficult for you." Alicia was solicitous.

"You know, I begin to see why your father spends most of his time abroad," he responded. "I daresay he prefers continual foreign travel to trying to deal with you!"

"Oh yes."

He stared at her.

"Well, we are both strong-minded individuals, with decided opinions, and, though we love each other very much, we cannot seem to agree. So it is best we remain apart most of the time." She paused. "Not that I deny him the whole of England, of course. He enjoys traveling. When the war was on in Europe, he toured India for nearly a year. So you see, it is not all my fault."

Cairnyllan shook his head. "You are an amazing creature."

"You are not precisely commonplace yourself, Lord Cairnyllan."

Their eyes met, and they both smiled. "Do you think we might finish out our dance without arguing?" he wondered.

"Unlikely. But we might *try*."

"Good."

Silence fell. Alicia tried to think of some indisputable topic, and failed. She looked up to find the same perplexity in her partner's face. "It *is* hot, isn't it?" she asked teasingly.

He burst out laughing.

She smiled. "I don't believe I have ever seen you laugh so spontaneously. And I know I have never *made* you laugh. You are a very serious person, aren't you?"

"I?" He seemed surprised. "I am conscious of my duties, naturally, but . . ."

"And do you ever take time to think of *pleasures*, rather than duties?" As soon as she had spoken, Alicia wished the words recalled. She had been genuinely curious and had not meant the query as it sounded.

Cairnyllan grinned, but he seemed to read her reaction in her face. "I have had little time for such in my life," he responded. "Yet I believe I enjoy a joke or a bruising ride or a meeting with friends as much as anyone."

"You did not—do not think much of our London amusements."

"No. I'm not interested in empty chatter, and half the people I meet do not at all share my concerns. I see no reason to waste my time with them."

Alicia blinked. This was a new view for her. Though she had often felt bored, she had attributed it to the repetition of events. "But . . . if you became better acquainted with them, you might find interests in common."

Cairnyllan shrugged. "Doubtful."

She scanned his face. "You sound so certain. Have you never made a mistake in this area?"

Arrested, he met her eyes. Was she asking about his opinion of her? But he saw only curiosity in her gaze. Still, the question gave him pause. He had been shaken by some recent developments; for the first time, his judgments *were* wavering, and due to her. It might be useful to explore the subject.

But before he could form a reply, Alicia said, "Oh dear, we are about to argue again, I fear. However, I have thought of something we can discuss with no danger of acrimony." Her pale blue eyes sparkled up at him.

"What is that?" he could not resist asking, though he was disappointed at the diversion.

"Horses!" Alicia was triumphant, and he smiled again. "You bought Black Lady, did you not?"

"Yes. She is being taken up to Scotland in easy stages."

"I hope she will adjust to the cold winters. Will you hunt her?"

He nodded. "After she has been ridden a bit. She

requires delicate handling." For some reason he felt it important to add, "Our winters are not terribly cold. We are near the sea."

"The northern sea." Alicia shivered. "I suppose you live at the top of a great dark crag, with the spray dashing over your terrace whenever there is the least roughness."

"Of course," he agreed, smiling. "In a dread castle, with turrets and a dungeon liberally supplied with skeletons. My valet is, naturally, a hunchback."

Alicia was laughing too hard to speak.

"Marianne and my mother are forbidden to mention it, on pain of the most dreadful torments. And I dabble in alchemy."

"Enough! Enough!" Alicia gasped for breath. "You have given me my own again, and more. I thought you were not a reader of novels. Why, you might write them."

Cairnyllan was smiling broadly. "I have heard that much from Marianne and some of her friends. And I have twice had to bear my sister company in the small hours of the night, when she was terrified herself through reading such a book in her bed."

This picture intrigued Alicia; it seemed so unlike him. "And what is your remedy for such terrors?"

"Hot milk and common sense," he replied promptly, his face serious but his blue eyes dancing. "And I would add that our house is set well back from the sea, in a rather fine garden, and has no towers or turrets whatsoever."

"How disappointing!"

They smiled at one another, more in charity than they had ever been, and both were sorry when the music ended and the couples around them broke up.

"Would you care for some refreshment?" asked Cairnyllan.

"I should like some lemonade." Alicia put a hand to her hot cheek. "It *is* warm."

"Indeed." Smiling, he offered his arm, and they walked toward the refreshment room.

There they found Marianne mediating a hot dispute between two very young pinks of the *ton*. "I *beg* your pardon, sir," one was saying icily, "but the lady is promised to me for the next set."

"She is parched with thirst, you blockhead," answered his rival. "Let her finish her lemonade." And he turned his back, effectively cutting his opponent off from Marianne.

Alicia threw Cairnyllan a mischievous glance. The disputants could not be much over nineteen, and both were clearly aspirants to the dandy set. Their outrageously cut coats and high starched collars made any movement awkward, and argument nearly impossible. Even to speak to each other they had to face directly forward, for they could not turn their heads more than a few inches.

Marianne saw them. "Oh, here is my brother. And Lady Alicia. I must speak to them. I will dance with you later, Albert."

The two young men turned, glowering, and eyed the newcomers. But neither could dispute Marianne's pronouncement, so after a brief hesitation they bowed and stalked away. A continuation of their disagreement floated back in disjointed snatches.

Marianne giggled. "I didn't want to dance with him anyway. How ridiculous they are."

Her brother looked gratified.

"Why are the men my own age such *idiots?*" she finished, and Cairnyllan's approval dimmed.

"They have not acquired much polish," agreed Alicia. "But you must remember that they have been in town only a few weeks."

"Well, so have I, but . . ." Marianne stopped and grinned. "I should not judge them so quickly, is that what you mean?"

"Actually, I meant nothing. You are far more poised than most young men your age. I think that is often true of girls."

"There you are, Ian!" Marianne laughed up at him. "Have I not always told you so? You should let me guide *you* through the intricacies of the Season."

"I am some ten years your senior," he pointed out. "However, there may be something in what you say."

Marianne stared at him, astonished. She had expected a setdown.

"You have certainly done very well so far," he added, completing his sister's stupefaction.

Alicia looked from one to the other, smiling. Marianne was gazing open-mouthed at her brother, and he was looking thoughtfully at his feet. They seemed a very different pair from the MacClains she had first met. "I am going to get some lemonade," said Alicia.

"Here, take mine," responded the younger girl. "I don't want it." She kept her eyes on Ian.

Alicia did so. She really was thirsty.

Cairnyllan looked up, smiled, and said, "I beg your pardon. I offered to fetch you a glass of your own."

Marianne seemed unable to quite take this in. But the change did not appear to displease her. She was still watching her brother when a movement caught her eye. "Oh, here comes that ridiculous Albert again. You must help me hide from him." She linked arms with each of them and moved off. "Look, there's an anteroom behind that curtain. Come on."

She pulled them away before either could protest, and in another moment they were through the curtain and inside a small chamber furnished with two sofas. Marianne breathed a sigh of relief, bending to peer through a crack in the drapery and say, "He is going."

Alicia and Ian, however, had noticed that they were not the only tenants of the room. A couple was half reclining on one of the sofas, deeply occupied with each other. Indeed, they were locked in a passionate embrace and oblivious to any intrusion.

Automatically, Alicia and Cairnyllan each grasped one of Marianne's elbows. "I think we should go back," said Alicia.

"Come along, Marianne," commanded her brother simultaneously.

Turning to look at them, Marianne glimpsed the couple. "Oh!" She flushed a bit and giggled, then her blue eyes grew wide. "Mama!"

Thirteen

This exclamation reached the passionately embracing couple, and the three young people watched, transfixed, as Lady Cairnyllan and Sir Thomas Bentham disentangled themselves. Alicia had some trouble retaining her composure; it was so ridiculous that the MacClains should come upon their mother in such a position—like a French farce. Marianne seemed inclined to the same attitude, though she was of course more startled and embarrassed.

Cairnyllan, however, was flushed with outrage. Despite the gradual softening of his opinions in the last few weeks, he still thought of his mother as above such vagaries as human passion. Finding her in the arms of a—to him—total stranger could lead him to only one conclusion. "Villain!" he cried. "Blackguard! Release my mother at once."

"Lower your voice, Ian!" retorted Lady Cairnyllan. "Do you want to bring half the *ton* down upon us?"

His flush deepening alarmingly, Cairnyllan pressed his lips together. Sir Thomas did not move away. On the contrary, he put an arm around Lady Cairnyllan's waist as if to support her.

"Mama! And you have lectured me for being *fast*." Marianne's voice trembled with a combination of laughter and uncertainty. It really was very odd to see her mother being embraced by a stranger. She had never seen even her own father do so.

"Thomas and I have reached an understanding," answered Lady Cairnyllan. "I would have . . ."

"You sanction the attentions of this . . ." Cairnyllan appeared unable to find a label emphatic enough. "Do you actually tell me you willingly engaged in this libertine display? There is a ballroom full of people just beyond that curtain, Mother. Someone might have come in at any moment. Indeed, someone did come in! You have exhibited your lack of moral principles to Lady Alicia as well as your own children!" His irritation seemed to be increasing rather than diminishing. "Must you stand in that man's embrace?" he finished.

Lady Cairnyllan looked a little daunted, and Alicia felt sorry for her. She had been unwise, perhaps, in giving way to her feelings in such a public place, but she did not deserve this tirade.

Sir Thomas apparently agreed. "Take a damper, young man," he said, in a deep, melodious voice. "How dare you speak to your mother so?"

"I speak as she deserves, if she chooses to behave like a wanton. And as for you, sir . . ."

Hearing dangerous overtones in his voice, and also feeling his unfairness, all three women broke into speech at once.

"Ian, stop being a beast," said Marianne.

"I think, Lord Cairnyllan, that you are making too much of this scene," suggested Alicia.

"Oh, Ian, do be reasonable," begged Lady Cairnyllan.

They succeeded only in drowning one another out, and Cairnyllan and Sir Thomas continued to glare.

"As for *me*," said Sir Thomas then, "I have done

nothing wrong. I merely strove to engage the affections of the woman I have loved since I was a stripling. And I have been fortunate enough to receive a second chance, after I behaved like an absolute fool thirty years ago." He smiled down at Lady Cairnyllan, who responded timidly. "I ask no more of life."

Alicia found this very affecting. "Don't you see, Lord Cairnyllan, that this is the most romantic and natural——"

"I don't care for *your* opinion," he snapped. He was feeling confused, and in the turmoil of his mind he once again relegated Alicia to the ranks of corrupt Londoners. Though some part of him murmured that he was acting like an idiot, the convictions of years overrode it. His mother and sister were to be protected from the anguish and abuse he had witnessed from his earliest youth. He had observed only one man in the character of husband and lover—his father—and he had never trusted the role since. A flood of old memories dispersed the last of his common sense. "If you do not take your hands off my mother, sir," he said between clenched teeth, "I shall make you."

Lady Cairnyllan grasped Sir Thomas's hand where it lay on her waist. "Ian!" Sir Thomas smiled confidently.

Cairnyllan surged forward, Marianne hanging on his coattails to stop him. He grabbed Sir Thomas's upper arm and flung him away, then hit him across the face with the back of his hand.

"Ian!" shrieked both of the MacClain women, forgetting the crowd outside. Alicia put a hand to her mouth and tried to think what to do.

Sir Thomas stood very still, his lips set in hard lines,

his gray eyes icy. "You badly need a lesson in manners, you young whelp."

"And *you* intend to give it me?" replied Cairnyllan contemptuously.

"I do. My seconds will . . ."

"Thomas!" pleaded Lady Cairnyllan. Marianne began hitting her brother's broad back with her fist.

Sir Thomas paused, and considered. His expression remained bleak, but finally he shook his head. "You are right, Mary. I won't challenge him. But it is only for your sake." Lady Cairnyllan threw herself on his chest.

"Then I challenge you!" cried Cairnyllan. "Coward as well as blackguard."

Sir Thomas paled with the effort of remaining silent, but he did so.

"For God's sake, be quiet," said Alicia. It was the third time she had offered this advice, but the previous two attempts had been drowned out by the dispute. It was, however, too late. Even as she spoke, three young men poked their heads through the draperies, excited and curious.

"Did I hear a challenge?" asked one.

"It was," insisted another. "Plain as anything. Who's to fight?" He looked from Cairnyllan to Sir Thomas eagerly.

The intrusion of strangers subdued even Cairnyllan, however, and he replied simply, "Get out of here. This is a private matter." His voice was savage.

The newcomers blinked, then retreated, but Alicia knew that they would waste no time in spreading the story throughout the *ton*, with whatever wild embellishments occurred to them. "Oh, why would you not be quiet," she moaned.

"It was Ian who made all the noise," accused Marianne. "You are always such an *idiot*, Ian."

"And completely beyond the line," added Lady Cairnyllan. "You had no right to speak so, to me or Sir Thomas. I insist you apologize at once."

"Really, you are making a great fuss over nothing," said Alicia.

"Not nothing," claimed Sir Thomas, "but certainly an unwarranted fuss."

Attacked thus from all sides, and conscious that he had brought down the gossips on his own family, a thing he had always cautioned *them* against, Ian could not be rational. "My seconds will call on you," he told Sir Thomas. And before any of them could object, he strode from the room.

Marianne made an exasperated noise. "He is the most pig-headed, conceited, *unbearable* . . ."

Lady Cairnyllan gazed worriedly up at Sir Thomas. "You will refuse to meet him, of course?"

He frowned. "I . . . it is a deuced tangle. They will say I was afraid of a younger man."

"Who never should have challenged you in the first place," interrupted Alicia, who was growing angry. "He had no cause whatever, and so I shall tell everyone. Moreover, I shall tell him!" She followed Cairnyllan from the room.

"Oh, dear," murmured Lady Cairnyllan.

"Never mind." Sir Thomas patted her hand. "I will refuse him. It was galling for a moment, but I can face down worse than that for you."

The lovers exchanged a tender glance. Marianne sighed.

"Your mother and I are going to be married, you know," added Sir Thomas, eyeing her sternly. He was not in a mood to tolerate opposition from any Mac-Clain.

"I thought perhaps you were," replied Marianne. "I wish you very happy." Stepping forward, she embraced her mother. "I was only a little startled at first."

"Well, of course we meant to tell you in a suitable setting," said Lady Cairnyllan, slightly flustered. "It was just tonight that we settled things between us."

"Ah." Marianne grinned. "That was the reason for the way we found you, I suppose?"

Her mother flushed and looked down, but Sir Thomas smiled. "I think *we* shall get on very well, at any rate." He held out a hand.

Marianne shook it. "I'm sure we shall."

Alicia caught up with Cairnyllan in the front hall where he was waiting impatiently for his hat and cloak. In the short time since he had left the others he had partly regained his composure, but her appearance destroyed it once more. *Her* presence at the preceding scene had made it a great deal worse for him. He told himself that this was because she was an outsider, and a fixture of London society who might spread the tale. What he did not fully admit even internally was that he felt exposed and embarrassed. How often had he criticized *her* for behavior much less shocking than that his own mother had exhibited. The destruction of his most cherished prejudices had been witnessed by a victim of them, and a woman whose good opinion he was coming to value above all others, though he had not yet consciously acknowledged the change. It was intolerable. Cairnyllan felt like smashing things. He wished bitterly for his home and the wide empty moors. If he could gallop alone for the rest of the night, a half moon lending just enough light to see the dirt track, his mount's breath frosty in the predawn chill . . . but he was trapped in London instead. Turning his back on Alicia, he strode impatiently after the footman who had gone to fetch his things.

"Lord Cairnyllan!" said Alicia, whose annoyance was not lessened by this rudeness.

"What is it?"

"I wish to speak to you."

"I'm sorry. I am just leaving. If that *numbskull* of a servant will only bring my hat."

"Well, if he does not, you can challenge him." Alicia's voice dripped sarcasm. She walked around to face him. "It would be nearly as sensible as your recent actions."

"That is none of your affair."

Alicia's blue eyes flamed. The fact that he was right merely increased her anger. She had a right to intervene, she told herself, because of her liking for Marianne and Lady Cairnyllan. Their obstinate relative must be set right so that they did not have to endure such outbursts. That she herself had been the victim of several, and that they had hurt her, Alicia did not consider. "What exactly do you plan to do?" she asked, ignoring his objection.

The footman returned, and Cairnyllan silently put on his things. When he strode to the door without speaking, Alicia followed.

"What do you think you are doing?" asked the earl.

"I am coming with you. I do not mean to end this conversation until you understand your folly."

He slammed the door and faced her on the pavement before the house. "How dare you use such language to me?"

"You are acting like a fool. It is not my choice of words." They glared at one another. "What do you mean to do?" she asked again.

He turned and started off along the street; Alicia had to half run to keep up with his long strides. "Who will act as your seconds, if you persist in this folly?" she continued. "You have no close friends in London. And no one will wish to serve in a quarrel so absurd."

"I don't call it absurd," he snapped, evading the very real issues she brought up.

"That is because you are acting like an idiot."

"My mother's honor . . ." he began.

"Honor! You have dragged her name through the mud. If you had behaved like a sensible man, the gossips would not even now be speculating about her and Sir Thomas. Indeed, about your whole family. Don't prate to me of *honor*. Would an honorable man make arrangements to shoot a gentleman more than thirty years his senior?" Her voice was taunting, and she was so angry with him that she did not even notice the discomfort of cobbles under her thin evening slippers or the chill around her arms and throat.

Cairnyllan clenched his fists. He could not answer her. He knew she was right—in this, at least—and he could not defend his rash challenge. Yet neither was he ready to withdraw it. He was a mass of confused emotions.

"The MacClains will be the laughingstock of London," added Alicia, thinking to convince him.

This merely added to the flame. "Will we?" he snorted. "That would indeed be a disaster. We have such respect for London's opinion."

"*You* have none. But what of your mother and sister? Do you believe you can speak for them? Are you truly so arrogant that you think *your* conclusions must automatically be theirs? Or are their thoughts and feelings of no interest to you?" This question seemed vitally important to Alicia, though if given time to think she might have wondered at her burning solicitude for the female MacClains.

Cairnyllan saw plainly that he had put himself in an impossible position. But the weakness of his arguments did not alter his determination. Quite the opposite. That Alicia should not only reproach him, but be right, increased his rage tenfold. His face grim, he hailed a passing hackney cab. "I shall call on Sir Thomas tomorrow morning," he stated as he got in. "And I shall thank you to stay clear of my affairs." With a signal to the driver, he slammed the door and set off, leaving Alicia alone in the street.

On the chilly walk back to the ball, Alicia rehearsed the scene just past and cursed her ineptitude. She had allowed her temper to speak for her and of course done no good. If only she were given another chance, surely . . . this train of thought led to an idea that made her expression extremely thoughtful as she re-entered the crowded ballroom.

Fourteen

Alicia found it difficult to think of anything else during the remainder of the ball, even though she did not see the MacClains or Sir Thomas again. Gossip had indeed begun; however, the stories retailed by three people who spoke to her were so divergent, and so garbled, that she was not really concerned. The probable actions of Lord Cairnyllan, and the others' reactions, worried her far more. If he *did* insist on fighting, Sir Thomas might become angry enough to agree.

Her mood did not lighten on the drive home, and Lavinia eyed her warily and remained silent. Alicia went directly to her bedchamber and undressed, then sat down in an armchair to think. The paramount issue was what to do. She felt she could not simply let matters take their course; she had to intervene. But how? There was no one she could turn to for advice. Had her father been at home . . . but no, he would have laughed, or forbidden her to meddle. She would have to stop Cairnyllan herself.

He had said he would call on Sir Thomas in the morning, so she must see him before then. Yet that was impossible. It was now very late, and even if a note reached him first thing tomorrow, he was most likely to ignore it, knowing what she wished to discuss. She must catch him somehow—an idea came to her. She would wait outside Sir Thomas's lodgings until Cairnyllan appeared, and she would convince him then and there to abandon this ridiculous duel. It was a rather unconventional plan, but the more she considered it, the more satisfied she felt. He should not escape her.

This settled, Alicia climbed into bed. But she did not sleep. The immediate problem solved, she was now free to wonder why she was so intent on interfering. Repeatedly, she tried to push the question aside, telling that irritatingly persistent part of her mind that she was merely trying to help her friends, and that she was of course eager to prevent violence and scandal. But it retorted that she had known the MacClains only a few weeks, and that they could hardly be called good friends. Too, she had never become so exercised about the numerous scandals that had rocked the *ton* since her comeout. What made this one different?

The image of Lord Cairnyllan rose before her then—his ruddy hair and brows, his piercing blue eyes, the strong planes of his face. She pitied him, she told herself. He was about to make a dreadful mistake because of his own unfortunate childhood and unfamiliarity with London. Anyone would wish to help him.

But that annoying part of her again protested. Very few would care to help. Indeed, most would not. Moreover, the man had treated her shockingly. He was arrogant, hidebound, and infuriating, and he had made it clear he had no regard for her opinions or her feelings. She was mad to continue the acquaintance, let alone to rush to his aid.

Alicia shut her eyes and bent every faculty to stifle

this inner debate. She knew she had to act. If she was not completely easy about her motives, it did not change that certainty. So agonizing was fruitless. Far better to simply go ahead.

With this eminently sensible resolution, Alicia strove for sleep, but it was some time before it finally descended.

As a result, she woke rather heavy-eyed, and only just in time to dress and breakfast before ordering her town carriage and setting off for the street where Sir Thomas Bentham resided. Fortunately, she knew the address; one of her cousins had once stayed nearby and mentioned with some chagrin meeting Sir Thomas and being subjected to a lecture on the evils of overindulgence in alcohol. The cousin had been careful to avoid the house after that, and had described to Alicia the maneuvers necessary to do so.

She directed her coachman to stop almost directly opposite the door, ignoring his raised eyebrows, and settled down to wait. Cairnyllan could not approach the place without her seeing. And she would use the time to marshal her arguments.

This proved more taxing than she had expected. It was all very well, she thought, to decide to convince Cairnyllan he was wrong, but she had very little idea how to do so. She had not had much success in this line up to now. Frowning and putting her chin in her hand, she pondered. She must try not to get angry, first of all. That was invariably fatal. And she must not use the accusing tone she had employed before. What would appeal to the man, she asked herself, and realized that she must come to a better understanding of his character if she were to answer that question.

Her frown deepened. Ian MacClain was obstinate, she knew, and remarkably confident that his own opinions were correct. He was also blindly prejudiced in at least one area—the very one where she must attack him. Yet he was not completely unreasonable; she had seen him give way over several points when they had gone around the stables at Tattersall's and she or William had disputed his pronouncements. He had, in fact, seemed very fair on that occasion. Yet where it concerned his family . . . Alicia realized that she must approach their discussion *through* his family, for only thus could he be swayed. Leaning her head back against the carriage cushions, she considered various possibilities.

She was so engrossed that she nearly missed Cairnyllan's arrival. Not until he had climbed out of a hack and was walking toward the house did she see him. She had to scramble out and run across the street to catch him before he rang the bell. "Lord Cairnyllan!"

He turned, astonished.

"I must speak to you. Will you come and sit in my carriage for a moment? Please?"

He found his voice. "No. We have nothing to discuss." He rang the bell.

Alicia strove to keep her temper. "I believe we do. If you will only listen to me . . ."

A servant opened the door. "Sir Thomas Bentham," said Cairnyllan.

"I'm sorry, sir. Sir Thomas has gone out of town."

Both Alicia and Cairnyllan stared at him. This was one outcome they had not expected.

"Out of town," echoed the earl. "But he knew I . . . where?"

The servant looked taken aback by his harsh tone. "I don't know, sir. He informed me he would be away until next week."

"I shall write him a letter," decided Cairnyllan. "Have you pen and paper?"

"Well, yes sir, but . . ."

"Good." Cairnyllan pushed past him, forcing the man to step aside and then conduct him to a pleasant sitting room on the ground floor. Alicia hesitated, then followed.

"I shall write a note and leave it here," added the earl, seating himself at a small writing desk. "I require nothing further."

The serving man moved uneasily from foot to foot, clearly reluctant to leave this alarming gentleman in possession of the sitting room.

"Well, go on, man," said Cairnyllan.

With a worried grimace, he withdrew.

"You could have written from your own house," pointed out Alicia.

"I am in the mood to have this thing settled. As Bentham has been so disobliging as to run away——"

"He has probably been planning this journey for some time!"

Cairnyllan gazed at her contemptuously. "Indeed? I imagine rather it is an admission of guilt."

"Oh, you are impossible!"

He shrugged and turned his back, picking up the quill pen. "You will not wish to linger here, I suppose. *I* certainly do not encourage it."

She was, Alicia realized, in an extremely unconventional position—in the rooms of one single gentleman, alone with another. A lesser girl might have quailed. But Alicia had determined to talk to Cairnyllan, and she refused to abandon her mission for propriety's sake. "I will speak," she insisted.

Cairnyllan merely hunched a shoulder and kept writing.

She gathered her faculties, keeping her temper well in check. "You really are making a great mistake," she began. "You seek to protect your mother—your family—but in fact you are hurting them more than any Londoner possibly could." Seeing his pen hesitate, she pushed eagerly on. "No one pays much heed to the gossip of strangers," she told him. "Oh, people listen, and no doubt enjoy the stories, but it is rather like a game. They do not judge the subject solely by the careless talk of outsiders. I know this. I have observed the process numerous times."

Cairnyllan's lip curled. "A fine sort of 'game.'"

Alicia ignored him. "*But,* if a family member, or close friend, lends credence to the gossip, then it *is* believed, and it can be very damaging. Don't you see that for you to fight a duel to defend your mother's honor—a *quite* unnecessary duel—will make everyone think there *is* something behind it. You don't understand the consequences. People will cease to call; there will be no more invitations. Marianne will lose any chance of——"

"From what I have heard," Cairnyllan burst out, "the *haut ton* is riddled with scandal. And far worse than this."

"Not *open* scandal," replied Alicia. "As this would be."

He turned back to his letter. "We will go home again."

"Marianne will be bitterly disappointed."

"I don't care a damn what Marianne thinks," he cried, goaded.

Alicia raised her eyebrows. "And are you also indifferent to your mother's feelings?" she asked. "Do you not think she deserves a little happiness after the misfortunes of her life?"

"She was perfectly happy at home."

"Was she? Odd. When I first met her, I thought her a melancholy character—so subdued and shy. She seems much changed since she arrived in town."

"I can't dispute *that*," he said bitterly.

"And for the better," added Alicia. "Have you ever seen her so gay and eager?"

He looked down at the letter paper, his mouth set.

Seeing this as a sign she was making an impression, Alicia continued, "Sir Thomas is a very good man, you know. I have been acquainted with him most of my life, and I have never heard a serious complaint. He had an excellent record as a soldier, and he is known as a progressive landlord as well. He has a large estate in Kent. He is *not* a pink of the *ton;* he does not participate in any of the pastimes you find so degraded. He is intelligent, honorable, and very well-liked."

"A veritable paragon, in fact," sneered Cairnyllan.

"As close as one may come, perhaps. Your mother is very lucky to have captivated such a man."

"*She* is lucky?" He glared at her from under jutting red brows.

"And so is he, of course," added Alicia hurriedly. "They are a splendid match."

"Match?" This possibility did not seem to have occurred to him before. He fell into a daze.

"Well, why not? Is it so unthinkable?"

"Yes!"

"I don't see why."

"Everything was perfectly all right until we left Scotland," he burst out. "We were happy, the three of us. Oh, Marianne complained from time to time, but she was actually content with her home and the neighborhood society. Mother was herself."

Alicia was losing patience. "Have I not heard some rumor of a duel even there?" A thought occurred to her. "Was *that* you also?"

"No, it was not!" he replied furiously. "It was a pair of young puppies with cotton batting for brains."

"Dueling *is* ridiculous," said Alicia sweetly.

"*Will* you let me be! What right have you to badger me? You are not a member of our family. You are not even a friend. I know what is best for them, and I shall do it. If they will do as I say and——"

"You are behaving just like your father, you know," snapped Alicia. "You must have your way, no matter the wishes and feelings of others."

He stared at her, stunned.

"There is really very little difference between beneficent tyranny and malicious, if one is being tyrannized." This struck Alicia as debatable, and she hurried on. "You refuse to listen to advice, yet you expect *your* opinions to be treated as commands. I suppose your father was just the same. His own wishes were the most important thing in the world. Perhaps he even felt that his acts were for the best, too."

"How dare you!" The glare in Cairnyllan's blue eyes made Alicia retreat a step.

"It is no more than the truth!" But she stepped back again, regretting her lapse of control. She had vowed to keep her temper, and failed. Now, Cairnyllan was far too angry to listen to her.

Indeed, he had never been angrier in his life. To be compared to the man who had hurt him so early, and whom he blamed for all the family troubles during his youth, was tantamount to being called Satan himself. And yet worse—for that analogy might be laughed off; this one shook as well as enraged him.

The suggestion that he might be like his father . . . he rejected it with loathing. And any inclination to consider Alicia's points vanished. "Get out," he said.

The savagery of his tone made her blink, but she could not quite abandon her purpose. "What are you going to do?"

"For the last time, that is none of your affair. God save me from a meddling woman!" He turned to the desk once again, his broad back hiding the trembling in his hands from Alicia.

"And me from a domestic tyrant," she couldn't help retorting.

He sprang up. "I said, 'Get out!'"

"This isn't your house. You can't order me about." As soon as she spoke, Alicia cursed her inability to mind her tongue. The earl looked goaded beyond endurance.

"I can throw you out," was his reply, and he strode forward and gripped her shoulders so tight she nearly cried out with pain. Spinning her about and almost lifting her from the ground, he forced her toward the entrance. When he let go to turn the doorknob, she jerked away, but he encircled her waist with his free arm, pulling her tight against his side.

"You must have learned *this* from your father," she accused, her temper by now out of control.

Cairnyllan froze, still angry but also appalled at his own loss of control. He had never laid a hand on a woman in his life. Unable to move, he looked down at Alicia. Her pale blue eyes flashed with rage; several of her silver blond curls had come loose and fallen over her forehead, and her cheeks glowed from the exertion. Something in him turned over at such beauty, and without thought he bent and kissed her full on the lips.

Alicia struggled against his iron grasp and against a rising tide of response that made her want nothing more than to relax within it. Her sensations were those of their long-ago encounter in the ravine; the events of the intervening weeks had not altered them one whit, seemingly. At last, overcome, she allowed her arms to encircle his neck and gave herself up to the kiss.

For an endless moment, they remained thus, enraptured by their matching passion, then Cairnyllan stiffened and thrust her away. Alicia, dazed by the strength of her emotions, fell against the wall and rested there.

The earl stared at her, his brain whirling. It seemed to him that he must be somehow bewitched. This woman had just accused him of unconscionable sins; he had been goaded into a physical attack, and yet had ended up kissing her deeply and passionately. It was mad. And it must be her fault. She was, after all, everything he disapproved of. Thus conveniently forgetting his own gradual change of opinion, Cairnyllan backed several steps into the room. "Get out," he said again, his voice low.

Alicia's breath was still coming quickly. She was confused by his behavior, and her own reaction, but even more, she was hurt. "I was only trying to help," she said softly, all her strengthening anger gone.

"I do not require the 'help' of the sort of woman who calls at a man's rooms unchaperoned," replied Cairnyllan. "And who stays for half an hour with no appearance of uneasiness. But I suppose you are used to it."

His tone was so cutting that Alicia cringed. Her desire to argue was gone, and it was apparent that she could not sway him. She wrenched open the door and ran down the hall, out of the house, and across to her carriage, ordering it home.

Cairnyllan slammed the door savagely behind her and strode to the desk once again. But seated there, he merely glowered at the letter paper for a space, then tore it across with an oath and departed as well.

In the safety of her carriage, Alicia dissolved in tears. All the tensions and emotions of the preceding scene poured out, and she was helpless to stop. When they reached the house, she bent her head, threw her shawl around her throat, and ran through the front hall and up the stairs to her bedchamber, the servants staring after her. There, she collapsed on the bed and gave way to her grief.

It was some time before the sobbing died away and she felt able to sit up and take off her bonnet. As she did so, she caught a glimpse of her face in the dressing table mirror—reddened and blotchy with tears. She swallowed and fetched a fresh handkerchief.

Why did she continue to endure such humiliation, she wondered? Almost every time she spoke to that man, he insulted or belittled her. What made her try again?

Abruptly, Alicia remembered the first time they had met, the correspondence she had sensed between them, a match of abilities and temperament that drew her as no man had before. Yet she had been mistaken —hadn't she? When she joyously threw herself into that connection, he had rejected her as if she were mad. He did not feel it. He simply disapproved of her life and her character and would not see that she did not conform to his prejudices. The only subject they had ever discussed pleasantly was horses!

Despondent, Alicia rubbed her hot forehead. She

was a fool. Why could she not stay away from a man who did not want her? Then she remembered his kiss today. She had not invited *that*. It had been his doing entirely. This recalled other similar moments over the course of their acquaintance, and briefly cheered her. But the memory of his eyes as she left him crushed her again. He had looked almost as if he hated her.

This thought was so dispiriting that Alicia shivered. She must not *care* what he thought. Why must she go over and over such painful recollections? Searching for an answer to this conundrum, she was suddenly overwhelmed by the realization that she had not ceased to love Ian MacClain since the moment they met. The knowledge left her gazing bleakly into the mirror and wondering what in the world she could do.

Fifteen

The night did nothing to dispel Alicia's despondence, and it was made more acute by the fact that she had always been such a strong personality. She was accustomed to asking for what she wanted quite freely, and to receiving it, either through her position or her persuasive power. A situation in which she was helpless to do anything but make it worse was new. This had been one of the intriguing characteristics of Ian MacClain all along, she realized; he was the only person she had ever met who could oppose her will with equal strength. Even her father chose to avoid confrontation with her. Cairnyllan was indeed her counterpart. Had he been only a little more open-minded . . . but he wasn't.

Alicia tossed through the night, posing one course of action after another and rejecting each until she finally lapsed into fantasy. A host of "if onlies" paraded across her brain, and she imagined what her life would be now if the earl had felt as she did from the start. Not bliss. But every moment would be filled with the exciting knowledge that her complement was there, to join her favorite pursuits, to sharpen her thoughts by his agreement or opposition, to heighten her senses as she had seen he could. Theirs would be no syrupy sweet happiness—their interactions so far had amply demonstrated that—but who would want such banality, wondered Alicia. She had had countless adoring suitors, but never before had she encountered a man to match herself.

The vibrancy of this picture made its dissolution more painful, but Alicia's common sense soon asserted itself and pointed out that her rosy imaginings were just that. Lord Cairnyllan did not see in her the affinity she found in him. In fact, he was only too likely to depart for Scotland very soon, and she would probably never see him again. This thought made her leap out of bed, though it was still early, and hurry to her wardrobe. But before she was half dressed, she stopped. She could not go to him; there was nothing more to say, and he would no doubt refuse to see her. All was ruined.

Alicia might have felt better had she known how Cairnyllan had spent his night. He had returned home from Bentham's restless and irritable, and the routines of the household grated on his nerves so that he left it again almost immediately. Visits to his club and a chop house proved equally intolerable, and even a brisk bout at Jackson's boxing saloon did not entirely relieve his feelings. At last, about dinnertime, he started pacing the streets of London, hands clasped behind him, face grim. His size and forbidding expression kept him safe from the many perils of the night alleys; heedless of location, he walked through areas where gentlemen rarely ventured, and elicited no more than sidelong looks and shaken heads. A few of the street women dared to accost him, but when he noticed their blandishments at all, he merely waved them aside and kept moving.

Indeed, he was hardly in London. His mind was

leagues away, among the moors where he often walked ten or fifteen miles at a time. As a boy, he had discovered in this rambling a good way to think and an escape from the palpable signs of his problems. It had grown from a necessity to a pleasure with the years, and tonight, the steady movement calmed him as the hours passed. By midnight, he was thinking that he had not felt so well since he left home.

With this peace came a clearer view of recent events. He had been a fool to challenge Sir Thomas, he admitted. He would write and apologize tomorrow. Whatever he felt about his mother's character change, a duel was far too public a reaction.

This solution of the immediate problem led him on to deeper ruminations. Alicia's arguments were fresh in his mind, and he set out to consider and refute each. That he could not simply dismiss them, nor banish the image of Alicia's vivid beauty, he put down to outrage at her injustice.

Very well, then, he told himself, his scowl shaking a fledgling pickpocket to the roots of his soul, the question of scandal can be passed over. The duel would not take place. And as for Sir Thomas Bentham's character—that must be looked into later on. Perhaps he was everything Alicia claimed; she would know, after all, that her assertions were easily checked. But this left two vexing questions—his mother's happiness and his own behavior.

Lord Cairnyllan thought back. His mother's life had certainly not been easy, he knew. She had been isolated in a strange country at the age of nineteen, neglected and periodically abused by a much older husband.

Cairnyllan recalled his father's unheralded visits

vividly. There was never the least warning, merely a sudden incursion of plunging horses and mud-spattered chaise. His father, a large ruddy man like himself, would stride through the house shouting for ale, his family, his bailiff. He expected all to be in readiness for him, and for whatever cronies he chose to bring for shooting or fishing, at a moment's notice. Yet, even when the household was at its best, he was never satisfied. Nothing in Scotland could match London standards, including his wife and children. His visits were punctuated by long drunken nights when Ian lay rigid in his bed waiting for cries or the sound of blows, and the burning spurt of rage that hurled him out to face his father's temper, standing between him and a cringing servant, or Lady Cairnyllan. How he had hated them!

The earl shook his head and drew a long breath. He had not thought of those years in a long time; he had made a point of stifling such memories. Could his mother do so as easily, he wondered now? And had his notion that they were happy after his father's death been illusion? Their lives had been peaceful, certainly, and he had reveled in the sole possession of his estate and position. But what did his mother and sister have to rival these absorbing occupations? Nothing—he saw now. Marianne had retreated into deviltry of various kinds, and his mother had been increasingly taken up with her recollections of a happier past. A past she was now in a way reliving, he realized; yet this was real.

With a wrenching pain, Cairnyllan admitted that he had been blind to his family's true needs. Concentrating all his faculties on shielding them, he had refused to see that they also required the chance to exercise their own abilities, and even make their own mistakes. He could not stand between them and the world as he had done between them and his father.

This admission did not come rapidly. Cairnyllan wrestled with the idea for some time, trying various rationalizations and being forced by his own sense of justice to reject them. In the end, he was exhausted and dispirited; it was hard to find that his benevolent impulses of the last few years had been misguided, for he indeed loved his mother and sister deeply.

Having gotten so far, however, the earl was forced to consider Alicia's most hurtful accusation—that he had acted like his father himself. Here, he balked. He refused to equate his own loving impulses with the latter's careless coldness, no matter how mistaken he had been. It was *far* different, he argued with Alicia in his mind, to command another from love and from selfishness. And *he* had never enacted a scene such as his father invariably created.

Except with Alicia, he amended then, and the thought chilled him. Did he, in fact, have elements of his father, awaiting only the proper circumstances to emerge? Why did Lady Alicia Alston make him behave so violently? He thought back over the course of their acquaintance. It still made no sense to him. She had seemed one sort of woman, and then another, and he could not decide which was real. He was ready to believe that he had misjudged her, but what was the correct assessment? He still had no idea.

And yet he did, he had to admit. If he evaluated her solely on the basis of her recent behavior, he was forced to a favorable conclusion. And never in the course of the Season had he seen evidence that she allowed anyone the liberties she had allowed him at Perdon Abbey. The memory roused feelings so strong that he stumbled on a cobblestone. That kiss today had been the same. What could cause a well-bred lady to . . . in one blinding moment, he saw it, and was shaken to the depths.

She loved him! And he loved her, more than he had ever loved any creature in his life. This was the explanation for everything that had passed between them since the beginning. And but for his own stupidity, they could have joyfully proclaimed that love weeks ago.

Cairnyllan looked up, aware of his surrounding for the first time in hours. He must get to Alicia at once. But the street in front of him was unfamiliar, and gazing about, he saw no landmark that would lead him to known parts of the city. No obliging strollers were about in these early morning hours.

Looking at the stars, he made a guess and started moving again. But as his emotions calmed slightly, he was overwhelmed by the realization that he had no right to go to Alicia. He had treated her disgracefully. Indeed, he could not see how he could possibly face her again. She would be perfectly justified in scorning his apologies and protestations and sending him on his way. Had he not done something similar himself only a few hours ago? She must be cursing his name by this time. He had thrown her love back in her face—he grimaced at the memory—and had no right to expect anything. How could he have been such a pompous idiot?

At this moment, his agonies were pierced by the alluring smell of fresh coffee, wafting through the damp predawn atmosphere. It brought his head up again, and he followed it around a corner to a dilapidated wooden shed dwarfed by three empty hackney cabs.

Entering, he found the cab drivers standing

around a small fire on which a fourth man was brewing a large can of coffee. The smell revived him amazingly. "May I buy a cup?" he asked.

The men turned to stare at him. It was obviously unheard of for a gentleman to enter their sanctuary.

"I've been walking," he added, "and lost my way. I'd be grateful for a cup of coffee before I ask one of you to drive me home."

"Sure, guv'ner. Here you are." The fourth man held out a large, battered tin cup steaming in the cool air. "Like a bun as well?"

Cairnyllan realized that he had missed his dinner and was ravenous. "Yes, indeed. Two, if you can spare them."

The proprietor chuckled, revealing stained, broken teeth. "Oh, aye. I reckon I can." He winked at the cabbies, who grinned and nudged one another.

Uncaring, the earl ate the doughy buns and drank the coffee. It was scalding and very strong, and his spirits seemed to rise with each sip. When he had finished, he paid the outrageous sum asked without a murmur and engaged one of the hackneys. As he rode back toward the West End, he determined to call on Alicia as soon as possible. She could do no more than throw him out, after all. And perhaps she wouldn't. Shoving his hands deep in his pockets and leaning back on the greasy cab seat, Lord Cairnyllan began to whistle cheerfully.

Sixteen

It was, however, four hours before it was even remotely acceptable to make a morning call, ample time for Cairnyllan's ebullient mood to evaporate. Though he stretched his ablutions and choice of garments as long as possible, he still had hours to sit in the library and consider how Alicia would take his apology. There was no reason, he knew, for her to receive it kindly. And if she did, she might well dismiss him forever afterward. Perhaps he deserved as much. But he didn't want to think of such an outcome.

Thus, it was with a set jaw and very upright carriage that Cairnyllan rang the bell at the Alston townhouse at midmorning. Admitted to the hall, and then the drawing room, he remained rigidly formal, his uneasiness disguised by this facade. But it began to crack as the minutes stretched out.

Alicia, informed of his arrival while still at breakfast after a restless night, had fled at once to her bedchamber. She brushed her hair, and started to change her gown, then buttoned it again with trembling fingers, and finally stood in the center of the carpet and tried to nerve herself to go down. She was being ridiculous, she thought firmly. This was a man she had met numerous times; they had dined, danced, conversed.

Yet since yesterday, everything was changed, for she knew now that she loved him. If he had come to continue their dispute, she did not think she could endure it. At last, however, she could delay no longer, and raising her chin and letting her eyelids droop haughtily, she marched downstairs to the drawing room.

Not surprisingly, the meeting was extremely cool. Alicia was distant and Cairnyllan stiff. When they had sat down on opposite ends of the sofa, a silence fell in which the mantel clock and the sounds of passing carriages beneath the windows seemed very loud.

Alicia grew puzzled, then tremulous. What was he about? Why had he come—to sit and stare at her until she fell into a fit of the vapors? For his part, Cairnyllan was commanding himself to speak and stop being an idiot. Yet words did not form in his mind. He gazed at Alicia, fascinated by her beauty and frightened by the thought that he might never see it again after today.

"Was there something you wished to discuss?" asked Alicia finally, unable to bear the silence. Her voice sounded high and unnatural in her ears.

"Yes," he replied, tension making his tone abrupt and harsh.

She looked at him, eyebrows raised.

"I have come to apologize," Cairnyllan forced out.

"Apologize?" Alicia was so surprised, she could only repeat the word.

"Yes. You were quite right about the duel, of course. It was a ridiculous notion; I shall drop it entirely. And . . ." He faltered again, then rushed on.

"I must apologize to you as well. I had formed a mistaken idea of your character early in our acquaintance, and treated you according to it. I . . . am sorry for the pain this must have caused you." He felt this to be lame, but could not think how to better it.

Whatever Alicia had expected, it was not this. Her cheeks crimsoned as she thought of the occasion that had given him the incorrect impression, then paled when she met his eyes and saw the intensity burning there. Her throat was tight, but she must speak. "I . . . I was partly responsible for your mistake," she choked out. "I was . . . I never before . . ." She trailed off; it was impossible to explain her feelings then, or now, to him.

Her confusion gave him hope. "I too have behaved in uncharacteristic ways with you," he offered. "Yesterday, for example, I was inexcusably rude—more than rude. Can you forgive me?"

The memory of their kiss in both their eyes, they gazed at each other in silence for a long moment. Then Alicia nodded and looked away; she could not speak.

The earl longed to sweep her into his arms; he could see the trembling of her slight frame from where he sat. But he was still uncertain.

"Thank you," he added, and searched for a way to go on. "That would seem to settle things between us," he heard himself say, and cursed inwardly.

Alicia nodded again. He would leave now, she supposed. They would meet as before at the *ton* parties, perhaps dance, but the other dimension of their relationship would be gone. She felt a sharp pain at the thought.

I must either rise and take my leave or speak,

Cairnyllan was telling himself savagely, but he did neither.

They sat very still through a trembling eternity, each filled with a burning protest. Things *should* not end this way between them after all they had been through. Then Alicia's butler entered the room.

"Excuse me, my lady," Bates said, "but a footman has just brought this note, and he is instructed to wait for an answer."

"Oh." She took the folded missive.

Lord Cairnyllan stood. "I *must* speak . . ."

But he didn't get a chance. In the next instant, the room was filled with three small, yapping bundles of hair careening off the furniture and nipping at their ankles.

"Oh, dear. Oh, dear," cried Lavinia Alston, running into the drawing room in a flutter of shawls and reticule. "Bess! Boadicca! Alfred! You know you are not allowed in this room. Come here at once. Oh. Alicia. Lord Cairnyllan. Bess get away from Lord Cairnyllan's boot. Now, madam, away!"

Gazing at the seeming carpet of small dogs about his feet, the earl smiled. But when he turned automatically to share the humor he saw in the situation with Alicia, she was looking unreasonably irritated. "Lavinia," she said, "you promised to keep your dogs upstairs." Alicia's bitter frustration with the situation had been transferred to the spaniels.

"I know, dear. We were just going up. We have been out for a walk, you know, and . . . Alfred! Off the sofa, sir, this minute!"

Cairnyllan lifted the offending Alfred off the cushions. He understood Alicia's reaction. Indeed, he himself was unbearably chafed by their estrangement. But he could not vent his emotions on this innocent older woman. His sense of justice, and the habit of years, was too strong. He made a massive effort. "What fine looking King Charleses. I've never seen any so glossy and full-coated." He tried to smile at Lavinia.

"But if you *could* remove them from the drawing room," put in Alicia.

The annoyance in her voice made Lavinia start and scurry to gather her charges.

"They are not doing any harm," Cairnyllan had to say.

"They will leave hair on all the furniture," she retorted, "and they may ruin the carpet."

"They seem much too well trained to do anything of the kind." He did smile at Lavinia this time. She had reduced the animals to a silent row.

"They are," she agreed, unable to resist defending the spaniels. "At home, they come into all the rooms, and they have never destroyed anything."

"They have distinctive names," added MacClain placatingly. "What was this one? Boadicca?"

A flush reddened Lavinia's thin cheeks. "Yes. I have named them all for ancient kings and queens of Britain, for King Charleses are *royal* dogs, you know. No one can forbid them entrance to theaters or any public buildings, by order of King Charles the second."

"Indeed? You know a great deal about them."

His interest made Lavinia expand almost visibly. "I am one of the foremost breeders of King Charles spaniels in England." Her face fell. "Or I *was*. Before . . . that is . . ."

"Before you came to London?" guessed MacClain.

Lavinia nodded.

"It must have been very hard to leave your home, in that case," continued the earl. "I suppose you had kennels and were very busy there."

"Prodigious busy. But I never minded that, of course." She looked proud. "I developed that shade of coat you see in Bess. It is known all over the country. The Duchess of Bedford has bought pups from me more than once."

Alicia marveled. Lavinia spoke of her kennels just as other Alstons talked of Morlinden. But why had she never shown such enthusiasm before?

Lavinia was shaking her head. "It *was* difficult to move to town, but I felt it my duty. When one is needed . . ." She stopped and sighed, as if not certain about that need. "I so look forward to the day when I can go home."

Alicia could scarcely believe it. She had not been at all pleased to have a chaperone, and she had assumed that the objections were all on her side. Now, she saw that there were other points of view.

This brief, incongruous interchange had affected her deeply, in her already sensitized state. That Cairnyllan, in their present situation, could kindly question Lavinia, and show Alicia things about her that she had not discovered in years, was astounding. And she suddenly saw that she had not been particularly considerate of her older cousin during their association. Concentrating on her own feelings and reactions, she had never paused to think of Lavinia's. Various examples of slight rudeness or lack of sensitivity occurred to Alicia, and she flushed. She felt herself wholly in the wrong, an unfamiliar sensation. And for the first time since the gambling incident at

Perdon Abbey, she felt that Ian MacClain had behaved much more correctly than she. She had known for some hours that she loved him, but she would not have included the kindness and intuitive understanding he had exhibited just now among his sterling qualities. Now that she had seen them, she realized that he was more complex than she had thought, and even more admirable. She had seemed harsh and unfeeling in contrast.

Alicia blinked back tears. Everything was ruined. She could not speak to him now of love. He must be despising her selfishness, as she did herself. No wonder he had never wished to marry her.

"I must get the dogs upstairs," said Lavinia, herding them out before her. "Good day, Lord Cairnyllan."

When he had held the door for Lavinia, the earl turned back, feeling much less constrained. This homely interlude had warmed him, and he felt he could speak to Alicia now.

But Alicia, mortified, was unfolding the note Bates had brought with numb fingers, a defense against meeting his no-doubt accusing gaze. "It is from Marianne," she said mechanically. "She asks if she may go to the Gerards' ball with us as your mother has gone out of town."

"What?" Diverted, he took the paper from her and read it himself. "I was told nothing of this." He stopped abruptly, frowned, then crumpled the letter in his hand. "Your prediction has come true. They have eloped!"

This broke Alicia's preoccupation with herself. "Don't be ridiculous."

"Sir Thomas is gone out of town for a week. My

mother has left London without informing me. She has never done anything of the kind before."

"I am sure there is a simple explanation."

"Yes! I have driven her into an elopement."

He turned on his heel and strode out, Alicia just behind.

Seventeen

Cairnyllan objected to Alicia's accompanying him, but she ignored his protests, and he was too hurried to argue. They took a hack to the MacClain house, and Alicia waited in the drawing room while he searched for his family. It was some time before he reappeared. "Mama is indeed gone," he said. "And Marianne seems to be out. I hope she is not looking for me."

"Why not ask her maid?" Alicia suggested.

Nodding, he rang the bell. When the butler answered it, he said, "Will you ask Annie to step in here for a moment, please?"

The man looked surprised. "Annie, sir? But she's not in the house. She's out with Lady Marianne."

"Oh. Well, did my mother leave any message for me?"

The butler shifted uneasily. "No, my lord. I understood she was to be away for several days. The gentleman said——"

"What gentleman?" Cairnyllan snapped.

"Why, the, er, gentleman escorting her, my lord. I have not yet become acquainted with all the London gentry, but——"

"She *has* eloped!" cried the earl. "And it's my fault. I drove her to it."

The butler's mouth dropped open, and his eyes seemed ready to pop. Alicia rose and went to Cairnyllan, but before she could speak he said, "What did this gentleman look like?"

The butler described Sir Thomas Bentham.

"And they left yesterday morning, you say?"

"Yes, my lord. Rather early."

"I suppose my mother had luggage?"

"Yes, my lord."

Cairnyllan put his hands to his face and blew out his breath. "That's it, then."

"Thank you," said Alicia to the butler. "That will be all for now."

Looking back over his shoulder twice, the man left the room.

"I'm sure this is only a mistake," said Alicia then. "Your mother probably told Marianne where she was going and asked her to tell you."

He shook his head. "Where would she go with Bentham? And just after they had agreed to marry? No, I see it all. Mother was so upset by my stupidity that she ran away from me. Probably she thought I would make difficulties about her marriage. Or—my God, of course!—she was getting him away from the duel. She thought I meant to kill him!"

"Lord Cairnyllan! Ian! That's ridiculous. Your mother would never think such a thing."

"Oh yes, she would. You do not understand her as I do. There is something childlike about her, despite her years. She is very easily persuaded, and she has always worried about my temper."

"Well, Sir Thomas would certainly convince her that her fears were nonsense, then. *He* would not flee London to avoid you." Alicia spoke rather sharply; she felt his reaction was excessive.

Cairnyllan paused, frowning. "No. But he would have wished to save Mother from further upset. And perhaps he thought an elopement the best way for them to marry. A *fait accompli*."

"Sir Thomas Bentham would never countenance such a scandalous plan," insisted Alicia. "He is not that sort of person."

The earl was becoming a bit irritated himself now. "Where have they gone then? Why was I not told?"

"Perhaps your mother wrote you? Why not look in your bedchamber?"

He stared at her, then almost ran from the room.

In the short interval, Alicia tried to gather her wits to persuade him not to do anything foolish. She had seen that blaze in his eyes before, and she knew it presaged trouble. Her own concerns were forgotten in this effort to help him.

"Nothing," said Cairnyllan, coming back in. "I looked everywhere."

"What about Lady Marianne? Where is she?"

"Out shopping with her maid. I inquired."

"There! If anything had happened, she would surely not——"

"No?" He laughed shortly. "Marianne would be delighted at the idea of an elopement. I daresay she would agree to help keep it from me."

Alicia hesitated. There was a grain of truth in this, though she did not really think Marianne would agree to anything so dubious.

"I'm going after them," declared Cairnyllan.

"What?" She couldn't believe she had heard him correctly.

"I must."

"But . . . but they have been on the road a full day. You will never . . ."

"I don't care." He strode over and rang the bell.

"What are you going to do?"

"Catch up to them if I can. Apologize. And bring them back for a proper wedding. We can hold it at once."

"But Ian . . ."

"Say no more. My mind is made up." The butler appeared, looking avidly curious. "Have Traveler saddled and brought around from the stables," the earl told him. "Ten minutes."

"Yes, my lord."

"Ian, stop it," said Alicia. The butler looked as shocked over her use of the earl's first name as he had over any of the foregoing events.

"The matter is settled. I shall see for myself what has happened. On horseback, I have a chance of catching them. I will take my leave of you now——"

"Oh no. If you insist on acting like an idiot, I am going with you to see that you don't make a worse botch of things."

"Nonsense." He turned to the butler. "Well, man, what are you waiting for?"

The servant went out, with deep regret in his face.

"I *shall* go," said Alicia. "It will take fifteen minutes for me to change and get my horse."

"I shall be at the edge of London by then."

"Very well. I shall follow *you* as well then. Alone."

They glared at one another, each thinking the other unreasonable.

"There is no need for you to come," said Cairnyllan.

"I think there is. Who knows what you will do if you come up with them?"

"I have told you . . ."

"And I have seen how you behaved in the past!"

He turned away. "I mean to ride hard. You could not keep up."

"I ride better than you do. Remember who fell at Perdon?"

"That was not my fault!" he began hotly, swinging around. But the reminder of that incident made them both think of all that had followed, and their anger died. They stared at each other, communicating without words, and each saw something cheering in the other's eyes.

"Oh, very well. Go home and change."

She eyed him suspiciously.

"I will call for you, never fear. I could not travel with the thought that you might be straggling along behind me alone."

"I shall be ready when you arrive," she promised, and hurried out.

Cairnyllan went upstairs to put on riding clothes and throw a few items into a satchel. Shortly after, he was mounting outside the front door. "I don't know when I'll return," he told the butler. "Explain to my sister." And he rode off toward the Alston house, leaving the butler wondering exactly what and how he was to explain.

It was hardly half an hour before he had the opportunity to find out. Marianne and her maid returned, laden with packages, and when the butler opened the door and took some of these she asked, "Has my brother come in?"

"Yes, my lady."

"Oh good, where is he?"

The man cleared his throat. "I fear he went out again."

"What? Why must he choose today to be away from home?"

"I *believe*, my lady, that he was somewhat upset."

"Really, why?"

The butler glanced at the maid, then gave in to temptation. "He appeared to think that Lady Cairnyllan had, er, eloped, my lady."

Marianne gaped at him.

"Yes, my lady. Very odd, I thought."

The girl took a deep breath and blinked several times. "Come up to the drawing room at once," she told the butler. "Annie, have someone help you with these packages. You may put away the things we have bought." Her maid dropped a small curtsey, and she and the butler exchanged a brief excited glance before the man followed Marianne's rapid steps up the stairs.

In the drawing room, she tore off her bonnet and said, "Tell me everything that happened."

With some relish, he did so. As he talked, Marianne paced about the carpet, frowning and clasping and unclasping her hands. Occasionally, she would mutter some exclamation, but the butler rightly took these as rhetorical and went on. When he finished, she did not react for a moment. Then she said, "When did he go?"

"About an hour ago now, my lady."

She bit her lower lip. "What a great ninny he is! I suppose I must——" She broke off, thinking.

After a while, she appeared to reach a resolution. "Have the chaise made ready," she ordered. "And tell Annie to prepare to accompany me. We will need our night things, I imagine."

"Very well, my lady. May I inquire——"

"No, you may not!"

With an icy bow, he went out. Marianne stood still for a moment, frowning, then abruptly kicked the yellow satin armchair beside her. The act did not seem to relieve her feelings, for she next whirled and stamped out of the room.

Eighteen

An uncomfortable, tedious, pointless journey, Alicia thought several hours later, is a very good way to learn about a person. She was feeling far from charitable. After racing to her house and flinging on her blue velvet riding habit, she had only time to give Lavinia the most sketchy of explanations before the earl arrived and demanded she mount up. This might have been barely tolerable had they proceeded to ride hard on the trail of Lady Cairnyllan. Alicia still thought their quest nonsensical, but the thrill of the chase might have stifled her doubts.

They did not, however. They spent the rest of the morning and the first part of the afternoon trying one after another of the main London roads, describing the objects of their search and seeking news of their route. As they started with the north, because Cairnyllan was fixed on Gretna Green, they did not uncover any traces until well after noon. For it appeared that Sir Thomas and Lady Cairnyllan had headed southwest. Their description was confirmed in two inns along that road.

"You see," Alicia remarked on the second occasion. "They cannot be eloping. Why would they come this way?"

"There are rectors to marry them in all directions. They are not under age, after all."

"You might have thought of that this morning when we were scouring the Great North Road. In fact, you might have sent servants to do this questioning. We have wasted hours."

"Servants are much less likely to get information," Cairnyllan replied. He was keeping his temper better than Alicia during this ride.

"We shall never catch them now, you know," she retorted. "They are a day and a half ahead. Even on horseback, we——"

"You may turn back whenever you like."

This silenced her for a moment. Then she objected, "Alone?"

"I will hire a groom at one of the inns to escort you."

Alicia fumed at his calm and ready answers. She had no intention of leaving him to go on without her. "Why are you doing this, really? You must see you cannot succeed."

He considered. "I'm not precisely certain. At first, I was driven by the strong feeling that I must make amends before my mother took such a decisive step in her life. So as to start fresh, you see. Now . . ." He paused. "It may be I am simply using the excuse to get out of London and go adventuring." He grinned at her. "You needn't indulge my whim. I will hire you a post chaise if you desire it."

Alicia shook her head quickly.

His grin widened. "Perhaps you have something of the same feeling? Admit you were weary of the round of balls and parties. Is this not twenty times better?" He gestured at the countryside around them.

"I came merely to prevent you from doing anything idiotic," she answered. But he had touched some kindred chord in her, and she avoided his eyes.

"Of course." He laughed. "Only that could explain this *extremely* unconventional journey. I assume it is not your habit to travel unattended with a single gentleman." He was teasing her, but there were echoes of the past in his question that made Alicia fume.

"I am not! *You* cause me to behave in wholly uncharacteristic ways."

"Indeed? I wonder why that is?"

"Because you are so infuriating. You haven't the least vestige of polish or civilized manners."

"Even yet?" he responded cheerfully. "Then London hasn't ruined me."

Alicia glared at his smiling, carefree face, and her lips twitched. This ride brought back echoes of their first meetings and made her humiliations seem trivial. After a few moments' valiant battle with herself, she burst out laughing. "You really are impossible."

"And *you* are adorable."

Alicia almost stopped breathing at what she saw in his eyes.

"We shan't get a chance like this again," added Cairnyllan, "to ride off alone on a quest. Let us enjoy it to the full before we go home again."

"I believe you read too many fairytales as a boy," responded Alicia, but she smiled.

"Indeed, I always longed for a dragon and a fair maiden in distress." He flourished his riding crop. "I knew I should make an admirable knight."

Thinking that this teasing comment was more revealing than he meant, Alicia smiled again and nodded. "Very well. But if we *should* happen to find your mother, I hope you will remember that she is unlikely to need rescuing."

He shrugged. "Perhaps they have been attacked by highwaymen while on a country drive."

"Don't say such things!" Alicia could not help checking the road behind them.

The earl laughed. "I was joking. Come, let us see what our horses can do on this flat stretch." He spurred his mount to a gallop, Alicia just behind him, and in the lively minutes that followed, both thrust objections and worries aside and gave themselves up to enjoyment of the day.

The journey went better after that. They lunched at an inn on bread and cheese and apples and rode on into the afternoon talking and laughing at one another's jests. Alicia's earlier thought recurred. One could indeed learn a great deal about a man under these conditions. And the things she was learning confirmed her love for Ian MacClain. She even dared to think that perhaps all was not lost.

They got news of Lady Cairnyllan and Sir Thomas about midafternoon, at an inn where the older couple had stopped to lunch. By this time, Alicia was beginning to think that they should turn back. It was very well to talk of adventuring, but if they did not start home soon they would not return to London before tomorrow, and she was not unconventional enough to wish for that. But when she suggested giving up, Cairnyllan wouldn't hear of it. "It is scarcely two," he insisted. "We must go on a little further." And because she hated to disappoint him, as well as to end a wonderful day, Alicia agreed.

They rode on as the sun moved down the western sky, its light turning from white to gold and slanting into their faces. A mood of deep contentment descended upon them; they said little now, but each could feel the other's quiet happiness.

"We will inquire at that inn," said Cairnyllan, pointing to a low building ahead, "and if we find out nothing new, we will turn back. Riding hard, we can reach London before full night. We wasted much of the morning, remember."

He sounded reluctant, and Alicia threw him a grateful glance. He was clearly doing this for her. Had she felt his mission was important, she might have urged him to go on without her then.

The inn, The Green Dragon, was welcoming. Ruddy light shone from all the lower windows, and inside, the front parlor was paneled in polished wood. Alicia sank gratefully into an armchair. She was not used to riding so long.

"Yes, sir, madam," said the landlord, hurrying in wiping his hands on a cloth. He was short but very fat, and his round face glowed with perspiration.

"We are looking for some friends of ours," said Cairnyllan, using the story he had told all along the road. "They ought to have passed here yesterday. An older couple—the woman small and dark and the gentleman tall and slender with gray hair. They were in a carriage and——"

"You wouldn't be meaning Sir Thomas, would you?" interrupted the man, frowning.

"Sir Thomas Bentham. Yes indeed!" Cairnyllan threw Alicia a triumphant glance and leaned forward.

"You say you're friends of his?" The innkeeper seemed suspicious.

"From London," agreed the earl.

"Ah? Well, why don't you go on to the house then?"

"House?" Cairnyllan looked blank, then frowned.

"That is just it," put in Alicia quickly. "We have stupidly lost the paper on which my, er, brother wrote the direction. We thought we should never find our way."

Alicia's silver blond hair and pale blue eyes seemed to have a softening effect on the landlord. "I can tell you that easy enough," he replied, his expression lightening. "Many's the time I've delivered a cask or keg to Linden—since I was a lad and my father ran this inn. For the old squire was as open-handed as his son; the Fermors are all so, they say."

"I suppose that is why Sir Thomas enjoys visiting so much," replied Alicia before the earl could speak. She saw that he was looking both puzzled and annoyed.

The innkeeper shrugged. "It makes it pleasant, but a man can't help visiting his sister now and then."

"Of course not. Sir Thomas's sister is married to the squire?" Alicia glanced at Cairnyllan; he looked astonished.

"I thought you were friends of his," answered the man, suspicious again.

"Actually, we are friends of the lady who accompanied him," she admitted. "That is why we did not know the way."

"Ah, Sir Thomas's fiangsay. A very lovely lady."

"Yes." Alicia was trying not to laugh.

"Shall I point the way to Linden, then?" asked the innkeeper.

"I am very tired," said Alicia. "It was a long ride. Might we rest here a little while? And perhaps have something to eat?"

"Of course, miss, of course." The round little man rubbed his hands together and reeled off a list of the viands available. Alicia made her choices, and he hurried out again.

When he was gone, there was a short silence. Then, unable to restrain herself any longer, Alicia started to laugh. She put her hand over her mouth, but could not stop. Cairnyllan looked disgusted.

"Visiting his sister," she managed after a while. "A terrible thing indeed. How could he dare anything so shocking?"

The earl moved impatiently. "Why did my mother not tell me, then? If it was nothing but an innocent visit, why keep it a secret?"

"Because you had been acting so bearish. After the way you behaved at that ball, I should have done just the same."

"But——"

"Oh, Ian, I am sorry, but it is not a glorious adventure after all. Nothing could be more natural than for Sir Thomas to wish his 'fiangsay' to meet his family." She smiled. "I certainly hope they take the news more quietly than you did."

He sank into another chair and put his forehead in his hand. "So, I've been a fool again?"

He sounded so dejected that she could not agree. She rose and went to put a hand on his shoulder. "We had a lovely day."

Cairnyllan raised his eyes. "You did not say that this morning."

"No. This morning was . . ."

He laughed, and Alicia, relieved at his rapid recovery, joined him.

"So it has been a chapter of accidents all along," said the earl after a while. "I suppose we must eat our dinner and hurry back to London before your cousin assumes that *we* have eloped." He paused, waiting.

Once again, Alicia had difficulty breathing. She felt as if she couldn't possibly speak, yet it was imperative that she do so. "There is no question of that," she managed at last.

Cairnyllan shook his head regretfully. "I suppose not. But I must say, I've never relished the thought of a great wedding. All that fuss and bother. Must a duke's daughter be sent off with a flourish? Think how much better it would be to simply visit a parson and get the knot tied."

"How can you joke?" Alicia bit her lower lip and turned away.

"We could have the bans published this very Sunday. Or I will ride for a special license, if you like. We are both of age. You could return to town as my countess."

"Ian!"

Hearing real pain in her voice, he fell silent, then moved closer. "I beg your pardon. I thought that making a joke of the matter might make it easier to tell you what I could not seem to say earlier. I love you. Last night, I could not sleep at all. I walked about London thinking of you, and finally saw that I love you with all my heart. I believe I am the greatest fool in nature. I have loved you for weeks, but I was too stubborn to admit it."

Alicia drew her breath in sharply, all her fears of the morning dissolving. "But you know I loved you almost from the moment we met!"

"Can you still? After the way I have behaved?" He held out a hand.

"Yes," murmured Alicia, too happy to think of the past.

In an instant he had pulled her into his arms. At first they merely clung together, like two people who have survived some deadly peril. Then slowly, as each realized that the uncertainty was past, they relaxed.

Alicia raised her head from his shoulder and met his eyes, and Cairnyllan bent his head and kissed her.

It was both like and unlike their previous embraces. The passion was there and the white heat of emotion. But a new element had been added, Alicia was flooded with a happiness greater than any she had ever felt. It seemed as she gave herself up to the kiss that nothing could go wrong for her again. And though she knew this was illusion, she reveled in the rising joy.

The earl too was elated. He could scarcely believe in his luck after the blunders he had made. He kissed her eyelids, her silver blond hair, her cheeks, then captured her lips again, feeling the eager response along the length of her body. He had not imagined he could feel this mixture of desire and tenderness.

It was some time before they drew apart and faced one another again. Both were flushed and breathing quickly, eyes shining. What they saw in each other's faces made them smile. "Will you marry me?" asked the earl, as if completing some superfluous form. "Will you come and live in Scotland?"

"Oh, no," replied Alicia with a smile.

"What?" He stared at her, thunderstruck.

"I will not *live* in Scotland. I shall be happy to stay there a large part of the year, but I must also watch over Morlinden, and I insist on spending at least a portion of the Season in town." She grinned impishly.

He closed his eyes and let out his breath. *"Don't* do that again."

Alicia laughed. "I'm sorry. Of course I will marry you. You may recall that *I* first suggested it."

"I prefer not to, for then I must also remember that I behaved like a coxcomb."

"Yes, you did," agreed Alicia cheerfully.

"Must we recall it?"

"I think it will be an extremely useful reminder whenever you begin to issue commands, as you are prone to do. I shall simply look thoughtful and murmur, 'An offer of marriage.' I daresay that will give you pause."

He laughed. "Doubtless. You mean to keep me in my place, is that it?"

"Yes." She smiled. "But I think you will like the place. And I shall have mine as well, of course. Side by side."

"I cannot believe it," he said wonderingly. "It is far more than I deserve."

"Nonsense! And even if it were, *I* deserve it!" She laughed up at him, eyes dancing.

"You do." He smiled also, but his tone was serious.

"Even though I am a shameless Londoner?"

"My outlook on the *ton* seems to have been rather skewed. I would not have you different in any particular."

Alicia could think of but one answer to this. She raised her lips to his and was immediately crushed in his embrace.

Unfortunately, the parlor door opened at that very moment, the landlord and a maid bringing in their dinner. The fat little man looked from one to the other of them with consternation, and it seemed for a moment that he would flee.

"Ah, food," said Cairnyllan. "Just what we want, eh, 'Sister'?"

Choking back laughter, Alicia agreed, and in a few moments they were seated opposite one another at a small table before the fireplace and being served with roast chicken and vegetables and a tolerable wine.

"You will never be able to visit your mother here," said Alicia when the servants had left them. "It is lucky this is not Sir Thomas's neighborhood."

"The man will forget us in a day."

"I doubt it. That will teach you to joke about eloping!"

"It is just that Gretna Green is so close to my home," he offered. "The thought inevitably occurs."

Alicia pretended to throw the salt cellar at him. "If you do not stop it," she threatened, "we shall be married in Westminster Abbey, with my father and all the other peers in their ermine cloaks and a show of fireworks over the Thames."

"Good God!"

They were laughing together when the sound of a carriage pulling up outside made them both stiffen and strain their ears. To be found alone together in this way by anyone who knew them would be fatal.

Voices passed along the corridor. They could hear the landlord, but could not make out what he was saying. The newcomer's tones were inaudible.

"He cannot bring them in here," whispered Alicia "This is a private parlor."

"It depends who it is, and what other accommodations he has," replied the earl. He rose, putting aside his napkin. "Perhaps I had better . . ."

But the door burst open, and Marianne MacClain strode into the room. "Here you are! Have you lost your minds?"

"Marianne!" they said simultaneously.

The girl looked from one to the other, then to the table and food. "Very cozy. I suppose I have made a tedious journey all for nothing? Have you discovered where Mama is?"

"At Sir Thomas's sister's," answered Cairnyllan a little sheepishly.

"Which I might have told you if you had stayed to ask. *Why* didn't you? And why did you tell all the servants that Mama had *eloped*?"

"I didn't!"

"You *were* shouting rather loudly," put in Alicia. "I expect they heard, or your butler told them."

"Of course he did!" agreed Marianne. "And probably half the servants in London as well. I have done my best to scotch the rumors, but I don't know how it will serve."

"He was being foolish again," said Alicia, her tone indulgent.

"And what of you?" replied Marianne turning. "Why didn't you stop him?"

"I *tried!*"

"And when you could not, you simply came along?"

"I thought I could prevent him from being even more idiotic."

"Did you? And so you have." She looked around again. "You have settled him to his dinner in the homeliest way." Abruptly, Marianne began to laugh. She put a hand over her eyes and laughed harder. She clasped her elbows and bent double laughing. Gradually, the other two started to smile.

"Are you hungry?" wondered Cairnyllan. "Would you care to join us?"

Marianne, speechless with laughter, merely nodded. The earl fetched a chair and ordered another place setting. By the time it had arrived and Marianne had been served, she was in somewhat better control. "You realize, Ian," she said in a shaky voice, "that you have been scandalously *fast*. I am shocked. It is obvious you need a chaperone desperately, and you are very lucky I arrived to play duenna."

Cairnyllan looked astonished, then amused at this reversal of positions. "I am indeed," he agreed, smiling.

Now, Marianne was amazed. "Lady Alicia, what have you done to him? He is being almost *reasonable.*"

Alicia laughed. "I rated him soundly, and as a punishment, I agreed to marry him."

"You . . ." The girl turned left, then right. "Are you bamming me?"

"No. We settled the matter just now." The earl smiled at his sister's expression.

"But this is . . . wonderful!" Marianne jumped up, rocking the small table perilously, and raised her glass. "A toast! To your engagement and many happy years. And to my new sister. How glad I am!"

Smiling, eyes bright, they all drank.

"And to our dragon of a chaperone," added the earl, raising his glass to Marianne. Laughing, they drank again.

It was a very merry meal. They agreed that tomorrow they would go to Linden and make everything right with Sir Thomas and their mother. With Marianne's arrival, the tenets of propriety were fulfilled. She and Alicia would share a room. "Perhaps you can have a double wedding," suggested Marianne a while later. "Wouldn't that be splendid?"

"No, it would not!" declared her brother. "Why don't you go and ask the innkeeper about rooms, Marianne?"

"That is your job!"

He gave her a speaking glance.

She looked at Alicia, then back at him, and

shrugged. "Oh, very well. But I shall not leave you two alone for long!" And with a flounce of her skirts, she went out.

Cairnyllan approached Alicia, who had moved from the table to an old sofa against the wall. "Are you all right?"

She looked surprised. "Of course."

"You have been very quiet for several minutes."

"I suppose I am tired. We rode a long way today."

"Yes. And that is all?"

"I . . . I suddenly felt sorry . . ."

"Sorry?"

She looked at him. "That our time alone was over. I love Marianne, but . . ."

"I know." He sat beside her and slipped an arm about her shoulders. "We shall have many times alone in the future. Whenever we like."

She nodded. "But not like this one."

"No. Not like the first. We shall be old, dull married people then."

Alicia threw back her head, looking outraged. "We shall be no such thing!"

He laughed. "You know, the first time I realized something of my true feelings for you was at Tattersall's. We were looking over Black Lady, and I saw that you and she were much alike. You reminded me of her again just then."

Alicia stiffened. "*I* reminded you of a mean-tempered filly?"

"Not mean-tempered. She merely needs the proper man to handle her."

Alicia drew back her fist and punched him in the chest, hard.

His breath came out in a gasp, and he looked

astonished. "What . . . was . . . that . . . for?" he choked.

"I am *not* some sort of half-wild creature to be 'handled.' What a despicable thing to say. Did we not agree to be equal partners?"

"I didn't mean——"

"Your meaning was obvious. And if that is the way you truly think of me, our engagement is at an end."

He met her blazing eyes, and held them for a long moment, his own puzzled and considering. He had really not thought to give offense.

"How would you like being compared to a great ruddy bear?" asked Alicia. "You grumble and growl alarmingly, but with proper coaxing you can be made to behave, and even dance." His red brows came together. "You see?"

"I think I begin to."

"Good." She paused, then went on, "I am not some sort of doll for you to watch over and protect, or cajole and master, Ian. You must forget that sort of thinking. Only look where it nearly got you! We neither of us need to do that sort of thing to each other."

"No." He was looking bemused.

"What is the matter?"

"I was just thinking what an extraordinary woman you are."

She smiled. "That's better."

They both laughed.

"I don't know why I have been so lucky," he added.

She reached up to touch his cheek, and he pulled her close. In the next instant, they were lost in a passionate kiss. Alicia's arms fitted automatically around his neck, and their bodies seemed made to mold together. Both felt a flood of desire combined with a glorious sense of rightness.

Neither was aware of the door opening, or of Marianne's head peering around it. She saw them before she could speak, and closed her mouth again. For a moment she watched, her expression pleased but a bit wistful. Then she withdrew. "Ten minutes," she murmured, her smile returning, "then the chaperone will have to put an end to these *scandalous* goings-on."

About the Author

Jane Ashford grew up in the American Midwest. A lifelong love of English literature led her eventually to a doctorate in English and to extensive travel in England. After working as a teacher and an editor, she began to write, drawing on her knowledge of eighteenth- and nineteenth-century history. She now divides her time between New York City and Kent, Connecticut.

JOIN THE REGENCY READERS' PANEL

Help us bring you more of the books you like by filling out this survey and mailing it in today.

1. Book title:_____

   Book #:_____

2. Using the scale below how would you rate this book on the following features.

Poor		Not so Good			O.K.			Good		Excellent
0	1	2	3	4	5	6	7	8	9	10

	Rating
Overall opinion of book..........................	_____
Plot/Story	_____
Setting/Location	_____
Writing Style	_____
Character Development	_____
Conclusion/Ending	_____
Scene on Front Cover	_____

3. On average about how many romance books do you buy for yourself each month?_____

4. How would you classify yourself as a reader of Regency romances?
   I am a ( ) light ( ) medium ( ) heavy reader.

5. What is your education?
   ( ) High School (or less)   ( ) 4 yrs. college
   ( ) 2 yrs. college   ( ) Post Graduate

6. Age_____   7. Sex: ( ) Male ( ) Female

Please Print Name_____

Address_____

City_____State_____Zip_____

Phone # (   )_____

Thank you. Please send to New American Library, Research Dept, 1633 Broadway, New York, NY 10019.